The Third Gift

by

David Armstrong

The Third Gift

Cover Art by *Kim Mendoza*

The Wild Rose Press, Inc.
PO Box 708
Adams Basin, NY 14410-0708
Visit us at www.thewildrosepress.com

Publishing History
First Young Adult Rose Edition, 2020
Print ISBN 978-1-5092-3213-0
Digital ISBN 978-1-5092-3214-7

Published in the United States of America

Mother sent Billy to bed that night without any supper, and I could hear him upstairs, crying and cursing and beating on things in his room with his fists.

Mother claimed Billy became possessed with anger after Sis died and told me to start praying for both him and Dad, so I did. I also prayed Billy would beat the devil out of anyone else who ever messed with me again, which he did.

I never thanked Billy for taking up for me that day. So later that night, after my parents had gone to sleep, I crept down the upstairs hall to Billy's bedroom, gently opened his door, poked my head inside, and saw he was sound asleep on top of the covers. Billy was still in his dirty socks and blue jeans, and he must have wiped his busted knuckles on his white T-shirt because it had bloodstains on the front of it.

I tiptoed across the orange-and-yellow shag carpet and slowly crawled onto the bed with him. I lay there for several minutes, rubbing his curly blond hair and trying to console him, since it was obvious he had cried himself to sleep. I wanted my older brother and best friend to know what he had done was okay and that he wasn't going to Hell or anywhere else for simply looking after me, no matter what our bossy mother had told him.

That night, I slept like a sheep next to its shepherd, and I prayed Billy and I would always be together. But this was a long time ago, and now it all seems like nothing more than a dream I had, once I was young.

Praise for *THE THIRD GIFT*

"A well-written, very human story of universal conflicts and outcomes. Readers who enjoy a good story, simply told, that reveals truths about human nature and the complex world we all inhabit, will come away with a lot to think about."

~Ronald L. Donaghe, author, editor, and publisher

~*~

"Every so often a rare novel captures the heart of the reader in many different ways. *THE THIRD GIFT* is just such a work that never lets go. Filled with wonderfully colored characters that keep you reading to the very end."

~Gary Roen, author, syndicated critic, and radio/TV host

~*~

Also by David Armstrong
THE RISING PLACE

Dedication

For Sharon Richardson—
the most beautiful soul I've ever known

Prologue

My father has always been a runner. When he was barely nineteen, after he had met my mother and had flunked out of Ole Miss, he was shot in the left buttock by a North Korean while trying to run for cover. According to him, he almost died, and the only thing that's kept him alive and able to sit on a commode all these years is Jim-Beam-and-Cokes.

I never saw my mother drink. She was a Southern Baptist from Tupelo, Mississippi, and my father was a Roman Catholic from New Orleans. A pretty good reason to not date and later get married, in my opinion—much less to have three children. But they never asked me. They asked my Grandmother Justice.

She told Mother she didn't approve of Catholics and to not marry my father, so Dad ran off and joined the Army under the pretense of saving South Korea from all the horrors of Communism. After the North Koreans sent him back to New Orleans with a big hole in his butt, he called my mother in Tupelo, swore he still loved her, and claimed he had found the Lord in a Presbyterian church somewhere.

Grandmother Justice told Mother she didn't believe my father and she didn't care for Presbyterians, either, but Dad convinced Mother it was "predestination" they get married. So they ran off together and did, and they later returned to Tupelo to live. There, they both joined the Presbyterian church, worked, fought, sometimes made love, and eventually had Billy, Sis, and then me. Grandmother was finally assuaged, but she said it didn't really matter since Dad was going to Hell for all the drinking and carousing he did—Catholic, Presbyterian, or whatever.

One Sunday, my father quit going to church. This was right after Sis died but long before we moved to Natchez. Sis's death must have hurt Dad awfully bad for him to run away from God. I'm sure Mother began praying extra hard for Dad at church. I would have prayed for him also, but I was too young then to understand loss and pain. This would come later.

I don't know if Billy ever prayed for Dad or not; I never asked him. Billy told me once he wondered where God was, especially when things hurt. Billy said he believed in God; he just never could find Him when he really needed Him. I told Billy Grandmother Justice said God was up in Heaven. Billy told me this was too far away.

I was only four when Sis got sick and died, so I really don't remember if I cried. Sis was eight, and Billy had just turned nine. They were barely a year apart and very close. But Billy cried. He cried a whole lot. This I *do* remember.

We never talked about Sis, only about her death. Mother said Sis's death was God's will. Dad swore it was old Dr. Bush's fault and wanted to sue him. I think some things just happen for no reason at all. This doesn't make things right or even logical. That's just the way life is.

But we should have talked more about Sis. I know now it would have helped us all. Especially Billy.

The four of us were sitting in our den on Thanksgiving afternoon when I was eight. Mother was reading about old Job in her Bible, Dad was drinking Jim-Beam-and-Cokes and watching a college football game on TV, and I was watching Billy build a great card house on the oval plaid rug on our floor.

It took Billy over an hour to get his card house built right, just like he always did. He sat cross-legged on the rug, staring at it for a few minutes, and then he smashed it flat with his right fist. No one said a word to him, but I couldn't believe he had done this, since Billy used to let his perfect card houses stand a day or two. Sometimes longer.

I realized then something was wrong, not just with Billy but with all of us. Mother went back to Job, Dad went back to his game, and I went back to my room and took a nap. Billy went back into himself. From there, he rarely withdrew.

But Billy was a great older brother to me, growing up. He basically took me under his wing after Sis died, and he always let me hang out with him and Marcus, his best friend.

I remember one Saturday morning, when I was nine, telling Billy and Marcus about this older kid around the corner who was fat, had pimples, and who had just whacked me over the head with a Wiffle Ball bat. When Billy heard about this, he told Marcus and me to stay put and rode his bike over to that kid's house. Billy caught him outside in his front yard, eating a Banana Moon Pie, and he beat him up for what he had done to me. This was the second time I recall noticing Billy's bad temper.

That afternoon, my mother got a nasty phone call

from the kid's mom, and she yelled at Billy for hurting him. Billy started crying and yelled back at her. Mother slapped Billy in the face and told him he was going to Hell if he didn't change his malevolent ways. Dad never said a word to Mother for slapping Billy and taking a stranger's side. Instead, he said he had to run get some cigarettes from the Mr. Quick store, and I think that's what hurt Billy the most.

Mother sent Billy to bed that night without any supper, and I could hear him upstairs, crying and cursing and beating on things in his room with his fists.

Mother claimed Billy became possessed with anger after Sis died and told me to start praying for both him and Dad, so I did. I also prayed Billy would beat the devil out of anyone else who ever messed with me again, which he did.

I never thanked Billy for taking up for me that day. So later that night, after my parents had gone to sleep, I crept down the upstairs hall to Billy's bedroom, gently opened his door, poked my head inside, and saw he was sound asleep on top of the covers. Billy was still in his dirty socks and blue jeans, and he must have wiped his busted knuckles on his white T-shirt because it had bloodstains on the front of it.

I tiptoed across the orange-and-yellow shag carpet and slowly crawled onto the bed with him. I lay there for several minutes, rubbing his curly blond hair and trying to console him, since it was obvious he had cried himself to sleep. I wanted my older brother and best friend to know what he had done was okay and that he wasn't going to Hell or anywhere else for simply looking after me, no matter what our bossy mother had told him.

That night, I slept like a sheep next to its shepherd, and I prayed Billy and I would always be together. But this was a long time ago, and now it all seems like nothing more than a dream I had, once when I was young.

It was also before my father got into trouble and we all ran away.

Chapter One

In May of 1978, when I was thirteen years old, we moved from Tupelo, Mississippi to Natchez, Mississippi. Mother had already been warned by Grandmother Justice that Natchez was a peculiar place and she probably wouldn't like it there. "Too many Catholics," she had claimed. My grandmother also said people in Natchez were "bad to drink." My father said this was good.

Tupelo was about two hundred ninety miles northeast of Natchez in an area of the state most Natchezians, I would later learn, referred to as "redneck country." But this term is misleading. People simply assume "redneck" means "country hick," "ignorant hillbilly," or some other Southern insult. But in my seventh grade civics class at Montebello Junior High School in Natchez, where I started the following September, I learned "redneck" was the description for the friends and supporters of an infamous ex-governor of Mississippi in the 1930s, Theodore G. Bilbo.

Our civics teacher, Miss Hattie Bowers, who was skinny and mean and probably never had sex, told us Governor Bilbo and his cronies always wore red neckties, so this is where the term originated. But Dad said ex-Governor Bilbo was a "horrible racist," red necktie or not, probably fearing the Lord's return for mistreating poor black people the way he had done, and to not pay Miss Bowers any mind. This was fine with me, since I hated civics anyway.

But I resented being called "the redneck runt from Tupelo" by this snooty rich kid who was in the eighth grade, so one day after school I busted his nose and broke his black glasses, and this was the end of that.

I remember the Sunday morning we moved from Tupelo like it was my first kiss.

Mother was talking to Grandmother Justice on the phone, and I overheard her say something about not believing our moving was "God's will." I wanted to tell her she was right, since it actually was *Dad's* will, but I knew Mother would have yelled at me for eavesdropping on her.

While she and Grandmother were discussing God and all the evil in Natchez, three black men were packing our things in moving boxes and carrying them and our furniture out of the house and into this huge moving van parked in our driveway. The driver had run a couple feet over onto our yard and caused a deep rut in the grass, since it had rained the night before. "An ill omen," I overheard my mother call it. Mother unloaded on the driver for doing this, but Dad told Mother to just forget about it, since our house was already sold. This made perfect sense to me.

I was wearing my favorite pair of cutoff jeans and an old T-shirt, which was filthy from packing and trying to help the three mover men. Dad had on a tight pair of blue Bermuda shorts, a white golf shirt, and the sweat-stained Yankees baseball cap he loved to wear. Mother was dressed like she was going to church instead of moving, but that's just the way she was then. Dad hated it when Mother would say, "You never know who might just drop by." But Dad didn't care about things like this. Neither did I.

As Mother and Grandmother continued to commiserate over the phone in the hall, I was standing on the last breakfast table chair that hadn't been loaded onto the truck, checking through all the kitchen cabinets to make sure we hadn't forgotten anything, and that's when I spotted it.

In the back of the left cabinet over the refrigerator, which went with the house, there was a half-empty fifth of Jim Beam whiskey. I couldn't believe my father had left it there.

I reached into the cabinet and grabbed the bottle. I almost took my first taste of alcohol then, but that didn't happen until the following summer, when I was fourteen and still grieving from loss and pain.

When I stepped onto the kitchen floor with it, one of the three mover men walked into the kitchen to get the chair. His eyes opened wide when he saw what was in my hand, and he asked me, "Where you gets that Beam from, boy?"

I told him I wasn't a boy and it was none of his business. Then he looked all around, reached inside the right pocket of his dirty jeans, and pulled out a crumpled one-dollar bill, which he swore he'd let me have for a quick sip of the whiskey.

His offer was tempting, but I figured my dad wouldn't have appreciated me letting someone else take a swig from his bottle. I told the guy, "No," and to keep his dollar bill, then regretted it later—all the way down to Natchez.

Dad walked into the kitchen after the guy had put the buck back into his pocket. When Dad saw I had discovered his stash, which he apparently *hadn't* forgotten, he snatched it from my hand and gave the mover man a "get-back-to-work" look. The guy picked up the chair, put it over his head, and walked out of the kitchen, mumbling something to himself about Dad.

I stood there feeling stupid and guilty. My dad was cool about it, though. He winked at me, bent over, and said, "Now, don't tell your mother about this, Charlie. Okay? She'll just tell your grandmother, and then we'll both be in trouble."

"Don't worry, Dad. I won't," I promised him. How could I? I had just foolishly turned down a quick, easy buck.

When the mover men had finally finished packing, loading everything into their van, and had already left for Natchez, I just had to go back inside to my bedroom and look around, one last time.

I slowly walked upstairs to my room. It seemed smaller, somehow more confining. It was the first time I had ever seen my own room naked, stripped of all my many things and memories. And it was the first time I had ever felt totally alone, like my parents and Billy had all just died or had run away without me.

I looked around for several minutes. It was hard for me to believe I had spent nearly every night in there for the past thirteen years but never would again. I recall this stark awareness made me sad, but what I like to remember most about that moment in my room is the warm summer sun showering through both my windows and the thousands of dust particles floating around in its rays, like tiny stars out in space.

I considered telling Mother she should have dusted my bedroom before we left for Natchez, but I knew

Dad would have said, again, to simply forget it since it didn't matter. And I'm glad she hadn't dusted it, because this last time in my old room is a cherished memory I'll never forget. I stood there remembering and watching the dust stars in the sun, but then Dad started honking the horn of our 1968 Ford station wagon outside. It was time to go.

I was also thinking about Billy. I regretted he wasn't still at home and going with us. Billy had just finished his freshman year at Ole Miss and was about to start summer school when we moved. I knew he was glad to finally be away from home, but I missed him terribly.

Then I ran out of my bedroom, ran down the stairs, slammed the front door behind me, and I never looked back.

Dad was sitting behind the wheel of our car, smoking a Tareyton cigarette, and neither he nor Mother said a word to me as I crawled onto the back seat. Mother was staring out her side window, and I remember seeing a tear fall from her eye and slide down her right cheek.

I didn't blame her, though. We all figured we'd never see our old house again. Then Dad checked his Swiss Army watch, sighed, and told my mother and me, "Take a good last look because we're never coming back here."

I would soon learn to never say never.

****

We had just passed a metal road sign, pelted with bullet holes, which read, Leaving Tupelo, Mississippi. You're Going To Miss Us. Mother picked up her Bible, lying next to her, and began reading in the Old

Testament about Job. She said Job was her favorite character in the Bible since he was so longsuffering, like her and Grandmother. Dad turned on the radio; Billy Joel was singing, "Honesty." He cracked his window and lit another Tareyton as he drove and sang with the song.

Natchez was in a remote area of the southwest corner of Mississippi, so I knew it would take at least five hours to drive down there. Mother stopped reading about Job, turned around, and looked at me. "Your grandmother packed a nice lunch for you," she said. "She put a Hershey bar in there, too. It's on the floorboard behind me, on top of my two jewelry boxes. So, eat."

"Thanks, Mother, but I'm okay now. I'll eat in a while."

"Suit yourself," she said, as she turned back around and pondered Job some more. I lay down on the back seat and began to think. This usually put me to sleep.

I was sad to be leaving Tupelo. I had always lived in the same town, gone to the same church and school, and had the same friends, so it didn't seem right to be running away. It also meant we were leaving Sis. I knew she was dead and buried and her soul was up in Heaven with Job, Jesus, and God, but I couldn't believe we were leaving her bones behind.

Grandmother had told Mother she would look after Sis's grave and not to worry, but I knew Mother would worry. She worried about everything and everyone, back then. Except for Billy. Mother had already given up on him.

Moving down to Natchez also meant being farther away from Billy and Grandmother Justice. Dad kept saying the change would do us all good, but I knew he really meant himself.

While I was lying on the back seat staring at the torn gray fabric on the ceiling, I thought about something dumb I had done when my parents and I had taken Billy and his best buddy, Canon Long, over to Oxford, Mississippi to start Ole Miss, the previous September.

We were helping Billy carry his duffle bag and suitcases up these tall, concrete steps to his freshman dorm when I accidentally dropped a heavy suitcase I had been lugging. It was Dad's old college suitcase when he attended Ole Miss before he flunked out and ran off to join the Army, and the thing burst open as it tumbled down the steps.

Talk about feeling like a fool! There were a lot of other students moving in that morning, too, and almost every one of them pointed at me and laughed. They weren't trying to be mean or anything, but my mother nearly had a stroke. She scrambled down the steps, started picking up all of Billy's clothes and stuff, and threw it all back in the suitcase.

Dad and Canon thought it was funny, too. I knew Billy didn't care, though, but only because he hadn't packed his *Playboy* magazines in the suitcase; otherwise, he would have cussed me and never let me look at any of them again.

Then I fell asleep.

Dad stopped our station wagon only once, at a Stuckey's south of Jackson, so everyone could go to the bathroom, get something to drink, and Dad could fill the car with gas and smoke a cigarette in peace without Mother complaining. Then we were back on I-55, heading southwest to Natchez.

I finally devoured the bologna sandwich, Fritos, and banana Grandmother Justice had packed for me, but I decided to save the Hershey bar for later. I was full as a butcher's dog, and I slept so hard on the back seat that I didn't wake up until we got to Natchez.

When Dad looked in the rearview mirror, he saw I was awake. He rolled down his window, threw his cigarette out, rolled it back up, and said to me, "Well, we're here, Charlie. Up and at 'em. We've got a lot of unpacking to do before it gets too dark." Mother nodded in agreement with Dad. This was a rarity, for her.

I rubbed my eyes and asked what time it was.

"Five-fifteen," Mother said.

It didn't seem like I had been sleeping for so long, but my stomach was growling, again. I reached over behind Mother's seat to grab the Hershey bar I hadn't eaten.

"Not before supper, Charlie," she said, looking in the rearview mirror.

"But, Mother, I'm starving!"

"Not before supper," she said, again.

As we drove into town, I saw a large wooden sign which read, Natchez, Mississippi, Where The Old South Still Lives! Dad honked the horn of the car when we passed it. I guess this meant he was glad to finally be there. Mother looked over at him and shook her head, so I figured she didn't agree. As for me, well, all I wanted to do was stop somewhere so I could go to the bathroom. Over-ripe bananas always did this to me—so did being jostled on the back seat of a ten-year-old car for five long hours.

Dad had already found a one-story brick house at 10 Melrose Avenue, which was close enough for me to ride my new bike to school. It was smaller than the two-story house we had owned in Tupelo, but Dad said it would do us all just fine. Directly across the street, though, was the biggest house I had ever seen. It was also old, needed painting, and the grass looked like it hadn't been cut in several weeks.

The moving van was parked in the driveway, so we parked our station wagon in front of the house. The three black men had already moved most of our things onto the front yard. The driver flicked his Kool cigarette into an azalea bush when he saw us arrive, and he drank the rest of his plastic glass of water. Then he hollered at the other two mover men to get their butts off our sofa before Mother saw them.

She did, though, and she said something un-Christian to Dad about "those two sweaty black men," sitting on her new sofa. I wondered if Mother would let me sit on it when *I* was sweaty, like my white skin would make my sweat not stink as bad. Dad didn't pay her any mind, though. He was too busy trying to see if the driver had driven onto our new yard and caused another rut in the grass by the driveway. Apparently, it had rained the night before in Natchez, too. The driver had caused a huge rut, and this time it mattered to my dad, even though we were just renting the place.

Dad and I got out of the station wagon, and I proceeded to check out our new world in Natchez. It didn't even *smell* the same as Tupelo, much less look or feel the same.

Dad walked across the front yard, making his way around all the boxes and pieces of furniture. He walked up the three brick steps onto our tiny, concrete porch, which had a black iron rail running down both sides. He unlocked the red front door with a key he pulled from the pocket of his Bermuda shorts. He opened the door and left it open so the mover men could start hauling all our things inside. Then he came back to our station wagon, started unloading it, and lit another Tareyton.

Mother got out of the car, and she and Dad started arguing about something. I assumed she was pissed about the men on the sofa thing and probably appalled that all our old, scratched furniture, except for her new but now defiled sofa, was scattered around the yard for nosy neighbors and people who drove by to see. She would never have admitted it, though—not even to herself.

Maybe she was just exhausted from riding two hundred ninety miles in a bumpy station wagon and commiserating with old Job. It seemed insane to me, and I felt sorry for Dad, since Mother was yelling at him pretty loud.

The red bicycle I had gotten for my thirteenth birthday in April was lying on the ground next to the van, so I went over and picked it up, walked it up the driveway, and leaned it against a wall in the garage. I walked back into the front yard, lifted the small mahogany table, which used to belong to Dad's mother, and this was when Tillman Dawes appeared, out of nowhere.

As soon as I saw Tillman, I knew he was nothing but trouble. He was this wild-eyed, lanky, pug-nosed kid with greasy red hair who looked to be about a year older than me. Tillman walked up and grabbed the table out of my hands, like a bully would do.

"Gimme the table," he ordered me.

I looked at him in disbelief. *Yes, sir, nothing but trouble here…*

"Boy, don't you know anything?" Tillman announced as he stared at me with his squinty, green eyes.

Just like Grandmother Justice always said. I glared back at him. *Trouble with a capital T.*

"Don't you know what this is?" Tillman asked me, as if I were a moron.

"What, this old table?"

"Yes, Einstein. It's a fine, valuable antique, that's what it is!" Tillman held the table up and examined it. "Probably just Victorian, a few scratches on it, but no big deal. You better let me carry it inside. You're just a boy. You might drop it or something."

"I'm not a boy." I wanted to bust his nose after he said this. "I just turned thirteen. How old are you, Red-on-the-Head?"

Tillman looked down at me and smiled, proudly. "I will be *fifteen* this November." He turned around and proceeded toward our front door, clutching the table in his arms like it belonged to him.

"C'mon, boy, follow me." He looked back and said, "I want to see how small this house of yours really is, I've been curious about it ever since Mr. Abrams died. He was a nice old Jew, but he never would let me inside. Strange, huh?"

Tillman followed one of the mover men, who was toting a large box on his shoulder, up the front steps and onto the porch, but he stopped and turned around. He motioned with his freckled face at the old house across the street. "By the way, that's my home over there."

Yeah, right, I thought. I turned my head across the street and gave his house a long look. "How old's that place?" I asked him.

"Old enough. Let's go. I don't have all damn evening to help y'all arrange things and decorate."

Tillman was standing in the den, admiring where he had just placed Granny Hall's "valuable Victorian" end table and directing one of the movers where to set a lamp, when I walked into our new house for the first time.

"Table looks great there, don't you think so, boy?"

"My name's 'Charlie,' " I said, "and I'm not—"

"This place is even smaller than I thought. How many bedrooms y'all got in here?"

He wasn't listening to me, and I really wasn't in the mood for all his bull, much less to bust his nose and get into trouble. "Two, I guess… Why?"

"Just two?"

"So how many bedrooms in your old house, Red?"

"Four. And for your information, Charles, it happens to be a fine, antebellum home—not just a house." Tillman showed one of the mover men where to set my dad's green Naugahyde lounge chair, and then he focused his weirdness on me again. "I assume you don't know what 'antebellum' means, huh, Charles?"

"Charlie, Charlie! No, I don't… Why?"

"Sorry, Charlie! Get it?" Tillman thought for a second. "Okay, then, where you from?"

"Tupelo. What's it to you, whatever your real name is?"

"Tupelo, huh? Well, hell, no wonder! My name's Tillman, Tillman Dawes. D-A-W-E-S, Dawes. So what's your last name, Charlie? Assuming you have one," he said with a goofy grin, revealing wire braces on nasty teeth, which badly needed brushing.

I was sick and tired of Tillman by then. "For your information, Tillman Dawes, it's Hall. H-A-L—"

"Yeah, yeah, I can spell. But I'll probably just call you 'Hall.' Sounds better to me than plain ol' 'Charlie.' "

I was about to tell Tillman to go home, but two of the mover men walked into the den and set our old RCA television in a corner of the room. Tillman sprang into action and told the older of the two black men he was obviously blind, since there wasn't a TV cable anywhere near there. Then he promptly directed them both to move the set to the corner near the front window, where he was pointing his long, skinny finger like the Ghost of Christmas Yet to Come.

With this task completed, Tillman strolled out of the den and went into the dining room. He sniffed the air several times. "Stinks in here," he said. "Did you just fart?" Then I followed him into the kitchen and watched as he began looking through all the cabinets and drawers. I assumed he was searching for forgotten whiskey, cigarettes, or dirty magazines.

"Hey, Tillman," I finally reminded him. "You never told me what 'antebellum' means."

"Huh?" He looked at me like he had no clue what I was talking about.

"Earth to Tillman, Earth to Tillman. Antebellum. What does it mean?"

"Oh, yeah, guess I forgot. They say geniuses do this a lot." Tillman looked down at me, put one of his long hands on my shoulder, and squinted his green eyes. "Listen, Hall," he said, "just so you won't seem like a stupid redneck, since you're living in such a cultured place like Natchez now, 'antebellum' means 'against women.' "

"What's an 'against women' home?" I asked him as the same two movers were now bringing our dining room table inside.

Without answering, Tillman walked out of the tiny kitchen, quickly examined the table, told me it was merely an inexpensive reproduction, and proceeded to instruct the movers to position it "squarely in the middle of the room, exactly under the hanging light." Then he praised both the movers. "Good job, men!"

The two black guys glared at Tillman, and the one who'd offered me the dollar bill back in Tupelo for a swig of Jim Beam said something about Tillman being a "skinny, redheaded, honky mother…" as they walked out of the dining room and into the den. I couldn't hear the rest of what he called Tillman, but I figured it was probably true.

As I was following Tillman back into the kitchen to get a mouthful of water from the faucet in the sink, he started bragging about his having this natural flair for arranging and decorating things, which he had inherited from his deceased Great-Uncle Oliver.

I hated to admit it, even to myself, but he did seem pretty good at this kind of stuff. I never told Tillman, since I didn't like to brag to strangers, but I had a "natural flair" too for hanging pictures, and it only took me three or four times to get them straight. So Tillman's flair didn't seem too special, to me.

"What's an 'against women' home?" I asked Tillman again as he was contorting his skinny neck under the faucet for a sip of cool water. "You never did explain."

Tillman gulped the water and then wiped his mouth with the back of his hand. "Damn, Hall." He shook his head and looked at me like I had just asked him his name again. "What they been teaching you up there in Tupelo? 'Against women' means our home was built by men who hated women. Duh."

" 'Duh,' what?"

" 'Duh' means you just asked a really stupid question. Listen, Hall, if you plan on making a go of it here in Natchez, you better start hanging out with me. Understand?"

"I'll keep it in mind," I told Tillman as I followed him out of the kitchen, through the smelly dining room again, and back into the den. "So when did these guys who hated women build your old home?" I asked him.

"I'm not really sure. I think about a hundred twenty years ago. My Great-Aunt Tillie says she remembers those days."

"A hundred twenty years ago?"

"No, Einstein, back when men used to hate women. Tillie said it all started after women got their right to vote, or something like that."

"Yeah, my dad claims that was a bad mistake."

"Well, whatever...but don't let Aunt Tillie ever hear you say something dumb like—"

"Wait a minute, Tillman—I thought you said she was your great-aunt?"

Tillman acted like he never heard me, so I assumed geniuses were like this, too. A mover man walked by us with a couple of large boxes and headed for my parents' bedroom, at the far right end of the hall.

Tillman glanced back over his shoulder at me.

"Let's go explore the hall, Hall!" he said. "Get it?"

"Shut up, Tillman. Okay?" I followed him down the hall toward our only bathroom, last door on the left.

Tillman walked into the bathroom and started looking around and sniffing the air, again.

"It smells like someone just took a dump in here. Bet it was one of those three mover dudes."

"Nah, they didn't have a key to get in the house. Toilet probably just hasn't been flushed in a while," I told him. "I need to, though."

"Thanks for sharing this information with me, Hall," Tillman said, sarcastically. He studied the murky water in the toilet for a few seconds, decided I was right, and then he flushed it. "Well, anyway, it stinks. You better call a plumber. There might be six months of crap trapped down there inside an old rusty pipe. Been months since poor old Mr. Abrams died."

Tillman walked up to the cabinet over the sink, opened it, peered inside, and then closed it back. "Nothing good in here, either. Needs a new mirror. I'd make the sellers pay for—"

"We're just renting," I advised him.

"Hmm, imagine that," he said, loud enough for me to hear.

I'd finally had enough of Tillman's nonsense. "Tell me about your great-aunt. What'd you say her name was again?"

"Tillie. I was named after her. She owns the home. I just live with her." He tugged at a few reddish, baby-fine whiskers on his chin, obviously in deep thought. "How come y'all only have one bathroom? We've got three. One down and two up."

I didn't know and didn't care. "Where are your

parents, Tillman? Why don't you live with them?"

A mover man walked past us, headed toward my parents' bedroom, as we walked out of the bathroom and went back into the hall.

"My parents are dead," Tillman remarked unemotionally, without blinking an eye. "They were both killed in a tragic plane crash. They were missionaries. To China."

"Oh, I'm so sorry, Tillman." I stopped in the middle of the hall. Tillman kept on walking. "I didn't realize—"

"Forget it," Tillman said, waving his right hand in the air. "No big deal. Besides, I never really knew them. I was only two years old when they left me all alone."

I followed Tillman into the den. He walked over to one of the front windows and looked out as my parents were finally about to walk into the house. Then he turned to me with a serious look on his face. "They never found their bodies," he said. "I don't guess they ever will, huh?"

Before I could answer him, my mother and dad walked through the front door and into the den, both holding boxes. They stepped aside as two of the mover men were struggling to bring Mother's tainted, green-and-gray sofa inside.

Dad put his boxes down and tried to help the older black guy position the front end of the sofa through the doorway. Mother stood there checking the place out, like she had never seen a small, smelly, cheap house before. Dad and the two men finally squeezed the sofa through the doorway, and then they walked over and put it down on the heart-pine floor, facing the two picture windows.

"No," Mother told all three of them, as she clutched her two jewelry boxes to her breasts. "The sofa needs to be put in front of the fireplace, not facing the windows. We don't want—"

"Good idea," Tillman interrupted. "I concur."

Mother glanced over at Tillman, obviously surprised by his quip. "We don't want the sun fading the couch."

"Duh? So just close the blinds," Tillman suggested.

Dad and the two movers hoisted the sofa and moved it in front of the fireplace, as Mother and Tillman had agreed. Mother watched them and told them to move it back and forth until they finally got it right. Then she looked over at me. "So, Charlie, who's your new friend here?"

Tillman folded his arms, cocked his head back, and spoke for himself. "I am Oliver Tillman Dawes, ma'am. D-A-W-E-S, Dawes. But I prefer you call me 'Tillman.' I live across the street in the antebellum home. I just dropped by to help y'all arrange things and decorate."

"It's an inherited flair," I added. "He got it from his Great-Uncle Oliver."

"Interesting," Mother said. "So, Tillman Dawes, that's really your antebellum home over there?" She pointed through the front windows.

"Yes. No. Well, actually…it belongs to my great-aunt. It'll be mine one day, though."

Mother put both her jewelry boxes down on the sofa, walked up to Tillman and me, and extended her right hand to him. "Well, it certainly is gorgeous. I'm Mrs. Hall, Charlie's mother." She pointed back at my dad and motioned for him to come over to meet

Tillman. "And this is Charlie's father, Mr. Hall."

Dad came over to Tillman, and they both shook hands. "Call me 'William,'" he said. "So you live across the street in that big old house, huh?"

"This is correct, William. It's been in our family for over—"

"It's an antebellum home, Dad," I butted in. "It was built by men who hated women—about a hundred twenty years ago."

"Well, I'm glad to hear times haven't changed much." Dad chuckled.

Mother didn't. "William, please. He might go tell his parents you said—"

"Oh, don't worry, Mrs. Hall, I won't tell my parents. They're both dead."

"They were Christian missionaries to China," I added.

Mother was at a loss for words, but Dad wasn't. "Well, this explains it, then. No wonder. Horrible people, those Chinese Communists! They hate Christians, just like those damn North Koreans who shot me in the butt," he claimed as he went over to help the other mover bring our coffee table into the den and position it in front of the sofa.

I looked at Mother. She was embarrassed. "Uh, Charlie, dear, why don't you tell Tillman you'll see him later. We still have a lot of unpacking to do." Mother turned around and noticed the young black mover about to put three boxes down in the dining room. "No, those go in our son's room—"

"Down the hall, first door on the left," Tillman quickly told him.

"Why, thank you, Tillman. Charlie, please go show

this nice boy where you want your things to go in your room."

"Hold up a second, Hall," Tillman said to me before I left the den. "I need to tell you something. It's important."

Tillman walked over to my mother and motioned with his head for her to lean over so he could say something to her. "Uh, they actually prefer to be called *men* now, Mrs. Hall. It's really not proper to call them *boys* anymore."

"I beg your pardon?" Mother shot back at him.

"And, frankly, it's redneck."

Tillman walked back over to me. He put his long, skinny arm around my shoulder and escorted me to the other side of the den. I glanced back at my mother. She was standing there looking like she wanted to throw rocks at Tillman and stone him to death. She put her hands on her waist and watched us like a hungry hawk.

"Do you believe in ghosts, Hall?" Tillman had leaned over to me and whispered.

"What? *Ghosts*?"

"Not so damn loud." Tillman glanced over at Mother. "Are you hard of hearing or what? Ghosts, Hall—do you believe in them or not?"

I knew then Tillman had to be insane. I whispered back to him, not daring to look at Mother again, since I knew she was about to scream. "No, I don't believe in ghosts. Why would you even think I did?"

Tillman got close to my left ear, like he was going to stick his tongue into it. He had putrid cigarette breath, just like Dad's. "Well, you just meet me tonight on the front steps of our home at twelve sharp, and you will." He glanced over to see if Mother was still

25

watching us. She was. "Can you whistle?" he raised one bushy red eyebrow and asked.

"Of course I can whistle. Why?"

"Just wanted to make sure, that's all." Tillman turned around and walked away while I stood there with a bewildered look on my face. As he headed for the front door, he walked past my parents and said, "Surely a pleasure to make your acquaintance, Mrs. Hall. Good to meet you too, William!" Then Tillman started nonchalantly whistling the melody to "Jesus Loves Me."

Dad looked up from one of the boxes he was unpacking on the floor as Tillman slid through the doorway past two of the movers who were carrying my parents' clothes inside, and then he vanished out onto our front yard.

Both my parents looked at me with a "who-the-hell-was-that" look on their faces. I stared back at them, shook my head, and shrugged. I neither knew nor cared.

At the time.

Chapter Two

It was amazing to me Mother was dressed like she was going to Sunday prayer service or to someone's funeral. With a linen tablecloth, real napkins, and two candles at both ends of the "inexpensive, reproduction" dining table, according to the bad-breath weirdo from across the street, you'd have thought we were having Dad's new boss over for dinner.

Just a bit too much, I thought. And I could tell Dad couldn't begin to figure how Mother had worked for three hours, unpacking boxes and arranging things, and then found time to bathe, dress, and set a formal table. Strangely, though, there was nothing to eat, so Dad went and got some food and drinks from Burger Chef. Mother insisted we all sit down to dinner, the first night in our new house. Who knows why? Like I said, that's just the way she was then.

I wasn't about to get dressed up for a Burger Chef bacon cheeseburger and a large fry. And apparently Dad agreed, though we certainly didn't plan it this way. So all he did was hop into the shower after he got back home, smoke three Tareyton cigarettes with his two Beam-and-Cokes, and then come to dinner wearing his old robe and slippers. I frankly had to admit this was ballsy of my father.

Unfortunately, Mother thought it was rude. After several minutes of eating in silence, I could tell she was about to pounce on him like a Tupelo tornado on a trailer park.

"I really do think you should have dressed for dinner, William," she finally remarked, without ever looking up from her plain hamburger, no pickles. "You never know who might just drop by, and we don't need to start off here like we're—"

"Yeah, I know," Dad mumbled through a mouthful of onion rings, never looking up either. "The only one who ever used to just drop by was your mother, remember? At least I don't have to worry about *that* anymore."

There was more silence. I could hear them both breathing and sighing. Dad coughed.

"Are you going to your new job tomorrow, William?" Mother finally asked him. "When did they say you could start?"

The tension between them was growing, so I tried to break the ice. "When do you get your new car, Dad? What kind do you think it'll be?"

"Probably, the first day I start."

"Which is...?" Mother inquired again.

Dad took a sip of his Coke through the straw. "Oh, I'll probably go down there sometime tomorrow, you know—just to check things out." He took a bite of his cheeseburger.

Mother looked like she had just heard Grandmother Justice was pregnant. "Do you mean to tell me they haven't given you a definite day and time to start? I don't believe this! I think you better call this Edgar fellow right now and ask him when you're—"

"He goes by 'Ed,' Claire—Ed, not 'Edgar.' "

"Whatever, William."

"And just how do you expect me to call him? The phones aren't hooked up yet, Claire. Remember?"

I immediately had a great idea, or so I thought. "Dad, you could use the Dawes' phone. I bet they have three or four over there! Why don't I run over and ask Tillman if—"

"Yes, no doubt they do," Mother told me, "but you're not going anywhere, young man. Finish eating your fries."

I did what I was told, though the fries were cold by then. There was something else I wanted to ask my father. My natural curiosity was driving me nuts, so I finally asked, "How much money they gonna pay you at this new job, Dad?"

"Well, Charlie," Mother interjected, "don't you remember us discussing this before we left Tupelo?" she explained. "With Billy at Ole Miss now, it takes more money to live on. That's why your father took this new job and we moved down here to Natchez."

Dad looked at Mother, and she got one of her "you-owe-me" looks on her face. So I suspected there was more to this story than my mother had just revealed.

"How much more, Dad?"

He pointed out the dining room window at the Dawes' antebellum home across the street. "Well, not enough to buy a big place like that, but—"

"Maybe one day, Charlie," Mother said, longingly. "Maybe one day…" Dad rolled his eyes at her.

Mother looked at Dad with an exasperated look on her face. "I do hope you'll stay with it this time, though, William. I really do."

"Now, Claire, don't start on me with all your guilt stuff. Not tonight, okay? I'm just too tired to hear it."

"I only mean I pray this move to Natchez was God's will for us."

"No, Claire, I know *exactly* what you mean, and it doesn't have a damn thing to do with God's so-called 'will.' " Dad got up abruptly from his chair and left the table.

"William, please, come back and finish eating your meal."

Dad walked into the kitchen and went over to the sink. He pulled out a near-empty pack of Tareytons and his Zippo flip-top lighter from his robe's right pocket, lit one, and exhaled several smoke rings toward the open window over the sink. He stood there smoking and staring out the window screen. Mother sat in her chair, slowly chewing a bite of her hamburger. I had finished all my fries by then, so I reached over and grabbed the last of Dad's cold onion rings.

"Claire, did you call Billy this morning before we left Tupelo?" Dad finally asked from the sink, without turning around.

"Yes, I did. I called him right before I called Mother and told her goodbye, about ten. I think I probably woke him up, though. He starts his summer classes tomorrow. He said to tell you hello."

"What about me, Mother? What'd Billy say about me? Did he tell you to—"

"Yes, Charlie, he said to tell you hello, too." Then she said to Dad, "I told Billy we'd call him again after we get our phones hooked up."

"Good." Dad thumped a long cigarette ash into the sink. "Did you ask Billy if he's still dating the same girl? What's her name, again—Ann, Anna Margaret…?"

"No, Ann Marie. I don't recall her last name. She's from Meridian. I'm pretty sure they broke up, though."

"I thought they were so 'hot and heavy.'" Dad took a quick drag from his Tareyton.

My ears perked when he said this. Mother got up from the table and brought her and Dad's dishes into the kitchen. I took one last slurp of Seven-Up through my straw.

"Actually, William," I could hear Mother tell Dad from the kitchen, "I hope they *did* break up. I never thought this girl seemed right for Billy."

"Kinda like your mother never thought I seemed right for you?"

Mother simply ignored Dad and looked back toward the dining room at me. "Charlie, if you've finished, get up and bring your dish in here so I can start washing them. And I need you to help me dry, okay? There's no dishwasher here."

"Yes, ma'am," I told her.

Mother leaned over to Dad, and I overheard her say, "Does Ed know about your accident? Have you discussed this with him yet?"

"Hell, no, and I don't plan to, either. Do you think I'm crazy? It's none of their damn business, Claire."

"But what if they find out? For God's sakes, William, they're an insurance agency—they're bound to find out sooner or later."

"Well, then, I guess it's just a chance I'll have to take." Dad snuffed out his smoke in the sink and walked out of the kitchen and into the dining room. On the way past me, he ruffled my scraggly blond hair as he headed toward the den to unpack the remaining boxes.

Mother followed him with angry eyes. "Don't you mean, *we'll* have to take?" she asked.

Dad walked into the den, knelt on the floor, and tugged at the duct tape on one of the boxes he had packed himself. Then he answered Mother back, "You worry too much, Claire. You really do. Just like your mother."

I'm not sure whether Mother heard Dad say this, because she didn't respond, but I knew then something was going on. I was beginning to get worried, myself.

Mother was too intent on stuffing Dad's cigarette down the drain so she could begin washing the dishes. After washing both their plates, she looked up and stared out the window screen at the Dawes' home, directly across the street. "What in the name of Heaven...?" she slowly said to herself. She looked back to the den and yelled to my father, "William—William! You must come in here—*quick*! You're not going to believe this! Please, hurry!"

Dad immediately got up from the floor and ran into the kitchen. He was carrying his grandmother Eglin's soup tureen he'd been unwrapping. I got up from the table with my plate and quickly followed him.

"What, Claire?" Dad asked, nervously. "What's the matter?"

I set my plate on the counter next to the ugliest yellow refrigerator I had ever seen. "What's going on?" I asked them both. Dad set the antique soup tureen down next to my plate.

Mother motioned for Dad to come over to the sink. She quickly positioned his head so he could see out the screen. Then she pointed across the street at the Dawes' front porch.

"Son of a..." Dad's eyes got big as ping-pong balls. "She's naked! That old dame's out there dancing butt-naked! Damn!"

Naturally, I had to see this. After all, I had never seen a live, naked woman before. The color photos of naked women in Billy's *Playboy* magazines and in Dad's *National Geographic* magazines were one thing, but this was the real deal! I ran to the sink and tried to push Dad out of the way. I figured he'd seen enough naked women in his forty-four years of debauchery and lust. But this, well...this was a first-time sin for me.

"Let me see! Let me see! Darn it, move, Dad!" I shouted at him.

"Trust me, son," Dad said as he refused to budge, "you really don't want to see this. This old broad must be seventy years old, at least. Who the hell is she, Claire?"

"Lord only knows," was all my mother could say.

I really don't care, I thought. All I knew was some woman was dancing naked on her front porch across the street. I had to see it. Seventeen or seventy—it didn't matter to me.

Mother moved me away from the sink. "I didn't get to see her! *Damn*! I mean, darn."

"Charlie Hall!" Mother looked at me and scowled. "Don't you *dare* use profanity in front of me, young man!" She ordered me to go stand by the yellow refrigerator.

"Sorry, Mother."

"Well, now, ain't this something," Dad said. "We've got a seventy-year-old exhibitionist living across the street. I'll just be damned." Then he quickly added, "Don't answer that, Claire."

"She must be Tillman's great-aunt," I advised them both. "He lives with her over there. He told me so."

"Well, she's a *nut*, whoever she is," Mother proclaimed. "Now, Charlie, I really don't want you to ever go over there, you hear me? You're grounded, if you do."

Dad was still staring out the window. "You know, she *is* a pretty good dancer. I have to hand her that, even if she is old enough to be your mother, Claire. She's graceful, too. Maybe she used to be a professional dancer? Or a stripper? Out there on her front porch with the light on, in front of God and everybody, just swaying in the moonlight, dancing and singing her old heart out. Claire, you're right, though, the woman's either nuts or drunk. Who knows, maybe both?"

"William, please, okay?" Then Mother looked at me. "I mean it, now, Charlie, I forbid you to ever associate with people like them or you're grounded. The *nerve* of this old floozy!"

Mother turned and looked for Dad. He had already walked out of the kitchen and into the smelly dining room without Mother ever noticing him. He kept on walking through the den and headed straight toward the front door.

"William? William! Where do you think you're going?" my mother called after him.

"I'm going out on the front porch to get some air, that's where!" Dad hollered back to her. Then he said to himself, but loud enough for me to hear, "They'll never believe this at the office. Damn, I wish I could remember where I packed my Polaroid."

Mother put her hands on her waist and called after

him again, "Don't you *dare* walk out of this house dressed like that, William Hall!"

Dad got his Yankees cap from the coat rack, put it on his balding head of light brown hair, and calmly said as he opened the front door, "Are you serious, Claire? With Lady Godiva dancing naked across the street—who the hell's gonna notice me?" Then he walked out the door and stepped onto the tiny front porch.

Mother was freaking. She stormed back to the sink. I made my break and darted out of the kitchen to join my father on the porch. Mother was still busy gawking through the screen at Lady Godiva on the Dawes' front porch. She never heard me run out of the house.

When I went outside, Dad pulled out a Tareyton, lit it, crumpled the pack, and stuffed it into the pocket of his robe. He shamelessly blew a huge smoke ring toward a magnificent moon.

And then I saw her: my first, real-live, honest-to-God, butt-naked woman. What a truly unforgettable sight it was!

Dad was correct, though. She did look old enough to be Grandmother Justice. But so what? Naked was still naked, at least to a thirteen-year-old, normal, horny kid like me.

After another minute or so of nude dancing, the old woman just all of a sudden stopped. She took a quick swallow from a small bottle she was holding, stood there for several seconds staring at the moon, and then she blew it and the world a long, dramatic kiss with her right hand, like I had once seen an old actress do on TV. She opened the front door and walked back inside. It closed behind her, and the front porch light went off.

The faded, lace curtains on her tall, left parlor

windows had been left open, and I saw her again as she closed them. Then she turned off the crystal chandelier in the parlor and disappeared into the dark.

I had left our front door open, and I heard Mother talking loudly in the kitchen. I figured she was still staring out the window screen and hadn't realized yet I was outside on the porch with Dad. "Thank God this Jezebel's finally gone back inside and turned off the light! I have a good mind to call the law on her!" Then Mother must have turned around and looked for me because I heard her say, "Charlie, I'm ready for you to help me dry these…Charlie? Charlie!"

I didn't pay Mother any mind, though. I remember thinking she could scream, slap me, send me to my room…whatever. I didn't care. My father and I were alone on the front porch, bonding and chilling out. And, looking back on this Sunday night in May of 1978, it was the first time in my life I recall feeling like my dad and I were "buddies."

Dad took a long, deep drag from his last smoke and then spoke into the muggy night air.

"You know, Charlie, I think I just might like it here. Sorta reminds me of growing up down in New Orleans and sneaking into some of those strip clubs on Bourbon Street when I was sixteen. Yep, these are my kind of folks, Charlie—my kind of folks."

"Me, too, Dad." I patted his back. "They're my kinda folks, too!"

Chapter Three

Sunday night, I was exhausted. It had been a tiresome, two-hundred-ninety-mile trip from Tupelo, not to mention all the unpacking.

There still were a few unpacked boxes scattered around my room, and my clothes were piled in stacks, here and there, but Mother had somehow managed to make my bed. So I stripped to my underpants, let all my dirty clothes stay where I had dropped them (which made sense to me, since a kid never knew when there might be an emergency, a fire, or some thief in the night), and then I hopped into bed. I lay in bed thinking about Tillman's naked great-aunt until about nine-thirty, when I finally dozed off to sleep.

Before I began fantasizing about Lady Godiva, as my father had kept calling her until Mother finally told him to shut his "lustful lips," I drank the rest of the RC Cola I had gotten from Stuckey's, but I never touched the Hershey bar, which was lying on top of my dresser, next to my watch. I figured too much sugar might overstimulate me, and I was already stimulated enough. I realized it was perverse to be thinking about someone's naked, seventy-year-old great-aunt, but the devil quickly reminded me first-time sins only happen once, so it was okay.

There was a full moon out, and it was hot and humid. I couldn't open my only window, since it didn't have a screen covering it, so I turned my ceiling fan on high. I didn't hear the twig rapping against the outside of the window, at first.

Then the rapping got louder and louder until something or someone started banging on my window and yelled, "Hall, are you dead in there? Wake up, man—it's after midnight!"

What the...? I sat up in my bed. Then it dawned on me: *Tillman*!

I got out of bed and turned on my nightstand light. I staggered over to the window, still half asleep, raised it open, and woke up as soon as I saw him. "Are you out of your mind? What are you doing over here, Tillman?" I demanded to know.

"Trying to wake your butt up!" He glanced at his watch. "You're late, Hall. It's already after twelve! I told you to meet me at twelve, sharp! Remember?"

"Man, you're nuts. Your whole *family* is nuts. I'm going back to bed. Goodnight!"

"I thought you wanted to see a ghost?"

"I never said I wanted to see a ghost! I don't even believe in ghosts, remember? You're weird, Tillman, you know that?"

"Have you ever seen a ghost, Hall? Huh? Have you? Well, I have—lots of 'em!"

"Aw, there's no such thing as ghosts, Tillman. That's just a bunch of—"

"Says who?"

"Says me!" I thought for a second or two. "Well, there may be *spirits*. We do have souls, you know."

Tillman began to crawl through my window, and I immediately regretted we didn't still live in a two-story house. "Oh, really?" Tillman said as he tried to straddle the windowsill. "So, what's the difference between spirits and ghosts? Same thing." Tillman caught his left red sneaker on the edge of the windowsill and fell onto the thin carpet with a loud thud. It was obvious to me Tillman had never climbed a tree. The guy was a total klutz.

"Man, be quiet—you'll wake up my parents down the hall."

"Nah," he said as he stood up from the floor and dusted himself off. "They're sound asleep. I just checked."

"*What?*"

"The blinds in their room were open. I advised your mom about this earlier, remember? We don't do crap like that here in Natchez, Hall. It's redneck."

"Yeah, well, in Tupelo—at least we don't dance around outside, butt-naked. That's *nuts!*"

"What?"

"Aw, forget it. Well…I guess you can come on in. I'm wide awake, now."

"Duh. I'm already in, Einstein. Hurry up and get dressed. You can't go ghost hunting in your pee-stained underpants."

I looked down at them; Tillman was right. "Listen, the only place I'm going, Tillman Dawes, is back to bed. I'm afraid you're out of luck tonight. So if you don't mind…"

Tillman followed me across the room to my bed. I got back in, pulled the sheet up to my neck, turned over, and faced the bare wall. Then I closed my eyes and prayed he would leave.

"*Hey,*" he said, "don't you want an adventure?"

"No. I've already had enough adventure for one

day. So go back to your old house and leave me alone."

Tillman reached over and yanked the sheet off me. He threw it down to my feet.

"Hey, man!" I growled at him. "I'm trying to get some sleep here!" I jerked the sheet back up, pulled it over my head, and turned quickly back toward the wall.

Tillman plopped his skinny butt down on the side of my bed like it was his own. "You're just a chicken, Hall."

"Am not."

"Are too."

"I'm not, you weirdo! Now go back to your nut house!"

"Nut '*home*,' Hall. Nut home. Remember? H-O-M…"

"*Shut up!*" I yelled at him.

There was silence for several seconds. Then he said, "Listen, Hall, just listen to me for a minute. Okay?"

"*What?*" I thought for a few seconds. "Well, all right—but make it quick. I'm sleepy."

"What if I told you there're ghosts, spirits, or whatever you want to call them, all over our home? Lots of them: male, female, young ones, old ones—hell, even black ones, for all I know. Anyway, they just come and go, come and go, all the time. And to see them, all you hafta do is ask Great-Aunt Tillie to make them appear. That's it! Then, when you want them to leave, all you hafta do is just whistle a religious tune, and they're gone. Poof!" Tillman snapped his dirty fingers. "Just like that! What you think, Hall?"

I thought Tillman was a lunatic is what I thought. I pushed the sheet down to my shoulders. I turned over and peered at him with a "yeah, right" look on my face. "Did you say all you have to do is just whistle some religious tune, and this makes them leave?"

"Just like that," Tillman promised. He snapped his fingers, again.

His fingernails looked like they hadn't been cut in six weeks. They were gross, and God only knew what all the black gunk was, caked underneath them. "Good, that's what I thought you said." I closed both my eyes and began whistling "Rock of Ages," the only religious tune I could think of at the moment. After a few seconds, I stopped whistling and asked out loud, "Are you gone yet?"

"Funny, Hall, very funny. Listen, I'm serious. This is for real—I swear it!"

I sat up in bed. "Man, you're *serious*, aren't you? You really do *believe* all this bunk." Then I studied him for a second or two. "You're not just messing with me, are you, Tillman, since I'm younger than you? 'Cause if you are, I'm gonna bust your darn—"

"Hell, no, I never lie—never!" He turned both of his palms face up and shrugged. "You do believe in spirits, right?"

"Well, yeah, sure, like I told you. But that's a whole different thing. Spirits are up in Heaven or down in Hell, not floating around some stupid ol' 'men-who-hate-women' home!"

"How do you know they're not, Hall? Huh? How do you—"

"I just know, that's all! Look, I really don't want to talk about this anymore. I'm going back to sleep now, so goodbye! And close the window after you leave."

Tillman slowly stood up from my bed. He looked

down at me and smiled as I stared at the fast-whirling fan and grasped the white sheet I had pulled tightly around my neck. His whole countenance had changed, and he had a look on his face like he felt sorry for me— like I was lying in a hospital bed, about to die. It's hard to explain, but I'll never forget it.

"No, Charlie Hall," Tillman said softly. "I'm afraid it's *you* who's actually out of luck tonight. I apologize for having disturbed you. I assure you it won't ever happen again."

This totally spooked me. It wasn't so much *what* Tillman had said but the way he had *said* it. It didn't even sound like his own squeaky voice. It sounded like the voice of some wise old soul. I lay there in bed and started getting goose bumps just thinking about it.

Tillman walked across my room toward the open window and crawled back out as gracefully as a gymnast. As he was retracting his right sneaker over the windowsill, I sat up in bed again and tried to get his attention before he left. "Hey, Tillman—does your Great-Aunt Tillie always dance naked outside at night?"

"Only when it's a full moon," he said softly, "only when it's a full moon." He closed the window behind him and vanished into the night.

Chapter Four

About the same time Sunday night, two hundred sixty miles northeast of Natchez in Oxford, where Ole Miss is, my brother Billy and Ann Marie (Mother was wrong: they *were* still dating, hot and heavy, just like Dad said.) were sitting at the bar in a smoky pool hall, which, according to Ann Marie, was Billy's favorite hangout. They were sitting there watching four drunk fraternity guys shoot a last game of pool. It was almost closing time, and most of the other students who had been there had already left for the evening. Summer school started the next day, as Ann Marie reminded us, the day my parents and I first met her.

Ann Marie had been sipping on a Miller High Life for a half hour or so, and Billy had been throwing down cold Budweisers like they were water. A young-looking bartender drying a glass with a towel finally looked up at the clock on the wall over the shelves stacked high with beer and cheap liquor, and announced to the nine or ten students who were still there, "Closing time, folks, almost twelve!"

Ann Marie said she glanced down at her Timex wristwatch her father had given her for graduation from Meridian High School, then turned around and set her Miller bottle down on the bar. "That's all for us," she told the bartender. Then she looked at Billy, who was still watching those four guys about to finish their game. "Billy, it's time to go. Classes start tomorrow." She claimed Billy acted like he never even heard her (a common thing, I've learned, most women swear all men do).

"Billy," Ann Marie asked again, tugging on the right sleeve of his Archie Manning jersey, "did you hear me?"

Billy finally turned around on the bar stool and looked at her with what she called a "highly inebriated" look on his face and asked, "Huh? What'd you say?"

Ann Marie pointed down at her wristwatch. "It's almost midnight. Time to go."

"Oh, yeah. Sure." Billy turned back around on his stool and faced the bartender, took one final swallow of his beer, set the can on the bar, and smashed it flat with his right fist. Then he chunked it into the trash barrel behind the bar.

Billy smiled proudly at the bartender, who had told Ann Marie he was in law school there, and gave the guy the thumbs-up sign. The bartender gave Billy a spontaneous thumbs-up back, and then Billy said, "How much we owe you, dude?"

The bartender handed Billy the tab. Ann Marie said she reached over and took it from his hand. "Let me buy tonight, Billy."

"Sure," Billy replied. "Hey, thanks, honey." Billy put his Ole Miss Rebel leather wallet back into his cutoff jeans and stood up from his barstool. He kissed Ann Marie on her lips. "Just gotta run to the bathroom before we go. Be right back. And don't tip him too much. Okay, beautiful?" Billy kissed her lips, again.

Ann Marie told us she pulled out a twenty-dollar bill from the purse Billy had bought her for her birthday and told the struggling law student to keep the change. The guy's eyes lit up at the prospect of a four-fifty tip, and he flashed Ann Marie a boyish grin, which said, "Thanks" without words.

One of the four guys who had been playing pool started racking his cue stick and noticed Ann Marie sitting alone at the bar. (Ann Marie said he had been checking her out from time to time, when Billy wasn't looking, but she had never returned any of his crude stares.) The guy winked at one of his drunk fraternity brothers, then proceeded to strut over toward the bar. He pulled his loose jeans higher up his wide waist, like he was John Wayne or something.

Ann Marie said she decided to just ignore him and turned around on her stool. She hoped the bartender was near so she could strike up a conversation with him about law school or some other mundane matter, but he was busy at the other end of the bar counting his tips for the night. She checked her wristwatch again and wondered what was keeping Billy so long in the men's room. *He must be talking with someone in there*, she thought, but she told us in the parlor she didn't recall seeing anyone else go in there before Billy.

The guy walked up next to Ann Marie, stood there, and checked her out for several seconds without ever sitting down. Finally, he spoke to her. "So the freshman punk left, huh?"

Ann Marie said she didn't say a word back to him.

He tried again. "The little blond-head twerp in the Archie jersey, sitting next to you. Did he split or what?"

Again, Ann Marie didn't respond.

"Hell, babe, surely y'all weren't *together*? That prick paid more attention to me and my frat brothers shooting pool than he did to you!" Apparently, the guy thought this remark was funny because he laughed and snorted out loud, Ann Marie said.

Ann Marie continued to give the guy the silent treatment, looked off again toward the bathroom for Billy, and glanced up at the clock on the wall. This must have made him mad.

"Hey, chick...!" the guy said loud enough for everyone in the pool hall to hear. "Are you deaf? I'm trying to make contact here!"

Ann Marie finally turned and looked at him. "My boyfriend is in the bathroom," she said calmly, "and I'm waiting on him to come back so we can leave. Okay?"

"Yeah, well, I kinda think the stupid runt ain't coming back, you know? So why don't you just leave with me?"

"No, why don't you just leave me alone."

It finally dawned on the bartender what was going down. He stuffed the last of his tips into his pants pocket and walked down toward their end of the bar. Then he spoke to the guy standing next to Ann Marie. "Uh, listen, friend, it's time for everyone to leave now, all right? I've got a torts class at eight in the morning, so I really need to—"

"Mind your own damn business, four-eyes!" the guy said threateningly to the bartender. "Me and Miss America here are trying to decide where we're gonna spend the rest of the night together." The guy then glanced over at his three friends, who were watching and listening to all this, and motioned with his fat head for them to come over and join in the fun. He leaned over to Ann Marie and added, "Oh, yeah, I almost forgot, my three buddies, here—they want to know if they can…?"

Billy had already left the men's room and heard everything that was said. Somehow, he had managed to slip around the side of the bar, out of John Wayne's sight.

Billy approached the guy from his blind side. Before he could get the next word out of his mouth, Billy grabbed him by the back of his greasy black hair and slammed his face down hard on the bar. Ann Marie said she clearly heard the guy's nose crack, and blood splattered on the right shoulder of her pink sundress. When Billy yanked the guy's head back, he was conscious, but his two front teeth were missing and probably somewhere on the bar. Billy then threw him down on the floor, jumped on top of him, and started pounding his face with his fists.

Ann Marie jumped off her stool and quickly got out of the way. She said Billy was wild with rage and she had never seen him like this before. The guy was screaming, and he was desperately trying to cover his face. Then Billy stood up and started kicking him in the ribs, over and over. Ann Marie said Billy just wouldn't quit.

Ann Marie was yelling at Billy, begging him to stop before he killed the guy. You'd have thought John Wayne's three buddies would have tried to help him, since he was getting the shit kicked out of him on a pool hall floor, or at least have broken a cue stick over Billy's head, but Ann Marie swore those three guys were terrified, bolted toward the entrance, and dashed out of there like Jesus' disciples in the Garden of Gethsemane after Judas and friends showed up.

(So much for disciples and so-called "buddies." Looking back, I can't say I blame those guys, though. Billy may have been small, but he could have whipped all three of them, too.)

Ann Marie told us she was panic stricken. The bartender had already called Campus Security by then, so Ann Marie grabbed Billy by one of his arms and pulled him away from the guy, who was writhing on the floor in agony. "Billy, stop! Stop! You're going to kill him, Billy! Stop it, please…!" Billy tried to break free of Ann Marie's grip and kick the guy again. "The bartender's called Campus Security! We must get out of here—*now*!"

Ann Marie dragged Billy toward the entrance, and Billy started cursing and yelling at the guy, who was crying and groaning, and bleeding from his face as he rolled around on the floor, clutching both his sides.

"*You sorry jerk!*" Billy yelled at him as Ann Marie tried with all her strength to force Billy to leave. "I'll kill you. I'll kill you! You *hear* me? I'll kill you the next time you—"

Ann Marie managed to force Billy through the door, but she didn't dare let go of him and try to close it. She feared Billy would break loose from her grip and run back inside to finish the guy off. She said the last thing she saw before she finally managed to get Billy inside her car and speed away was the bartender running around the bar to the fool on the floor.

When the bartender saw John Wayne's bloody face, he turned white as cotton, she told us. He tried to cover his mouth with his hands, and then he vomited as he started backing away.

****

Early the same morning, long before I had awakened down in Natchez, Billy was sound asleep and snoring away in his dorm room bed with his clothes still on. Ann Marie said she had snuck into Billy's dorm and had spent the rest of the night with him. She was wide awake and lying there next to Billy, watching him sleep. (I figured Billy and Ann Marie had been shacking up, but I would never have snitched on him.)

Suddenly, Billy started having this bad nightmare, she told us. (My mother called it a "night terror." She said Billy used to have them all the time, after Sis died.) Ann Marie said Billy's head started rolling back and forth on his pillow, as he moaned, "I'm sorry—I'm sorry! I did pray! I did pray! I *did* pray…!"

Ann Marie said she didn't have a clue what Billy had been moaning about. Neither did I, at the time. But when Mother explained in the parlor what Billy's night terror had been about, I remember her sighing heavily, dropping her head, and covering her face with her hands as she cried. My father cried too, and so did I.

But I don't want to get into all this. Not now.

Billy awoke and sat up in bed, gasping for air like he was choking. Ann Marie sat up too, almost scared out of her wits. Billy was staring across the room, as if he were in some sort of trance, so Ann Marie put a hand on his shoulder. "Billy, are you all right?" she asked him. "You were having a bad dream."

Billy never said a word. He got out of bed, ran across the tile floor into the bathroom, slammed the door, and locked it. And Marie told us she heard Billy vomit in the toilet.

Ann Marie said she sat there staring at the door, wondering what the matter was. She assumed Billy probably had a bad hangover and his stomach was upset. "Billy," Ann Marie called out to him in the bathroom, "are you okay?" She stood up from the bed, walked over to the door, and knocked softly on it. "Billy, are you sick? Let me come in so I can help."

"No, leave me alone! Just *leave…me…alone…*!"

****

Later the same morning, Billy was sitting in his second-year algebra class. Ann Marie said she was in a Mississippi history class in another building, across campus. While Billy's instructor was writing something on the chalkboard, a burly old Campus Security officer opened the door and wedged his big head inside. Canon Long, who was in the same class, told us the officer had a "cop-nose," which had obviously been broken a few times over the years, a head of flowing white hair, Popeye arms, and no neck. He also carried no gun, which, considering his imposing stature, came as no real surprise, Canon added.

The officer walked over to the obese instructor, who got this immediate, panicky look on his rotund face like he was about to be arrested (probably for all the pot he had been selling to rich fraternity guys to help pay his graduate school expenses, Canon revealed).

The officer handed him a piece of folded yellow paper from a legal pad. He opened it with trembling hands and began to read. When he finished reading the short note, he briefly closed both his eyes in grateful respite, nodded, and handed the note back to the security cop. The instructor, still trembling, pointed his left index finger toward the left back corner of the stifling-hot lecture room at Billy, who *did* have a bad hangover, was barely awake, and slumped over in the third row from the back, first seat from the left.

The old cop, who was probably an ex-Marine, Canon surmised, spoke in a drill sergeant's voice. "William Eglin Hall, Junior, get up and come to the front of the class. On the double, son!" Billy immediately sat up in his chair. Canon said he dropped his jaw when he heard this and noticed some old hulk motioning for Billy to get up and go with him.

Billy pointed at himself, raised his eyebrows, and mumbled, "Me?" Then he looked at Canon, who was seated next to him, and shook his head. "Shit, I'm dead now." Billy had already told Canon earlier that morning what happened, as he and Canon were walking to class, both smoking Winstons, and then a second time while they waited outside for the fat graduate assistant to show up for the class.

"Hell, man, like I tried to tell you before class this morning—that was Chancellor Wright's *nephew* you damn near beat to death last night! What'd you expect, Billy—the chancellor wouldn't find out about it?"

"Shut up, Canonball, just shut up, all right? I don't want anyone else knowing about this. You hear me? I can't have my folks finding out—my mother'd kill me. You gotta promise me, Canonball, okay?"

"Sure, Billy, sure. You know I will. But right now, I think you better—"

"Hall!" the officer bellowed, again. "Front and center, now! Don't make me have to come back there and get you!"

You could have heard a clipped fingernail fall to the wooden floor in there. Billy turned around, got up from his chair, and slowly sauntered toward the front of the class, Canon told us.

Billy's trepidation was obvious to everyone. There were no smiles on anyone's faces, no snickers nor pointing, and no one dared to say a word. All eyes were fixed upon Billy, and Canon claimed most of them were probably thinking thoughts like, "Dead man walking," "But for the grace of God, there goeth me," and surely, "Later, dude…"

****

After his chemistry class was over at nine-fifty, Canon was waiting for Billy outside the Dean of Students' office in the Lyceum, the one-hundred-fifty-year-old administration building at the upper west corner of the "Grove," a bucolic, sacrosanct site where students studied, played Frisbee, smoked a little dope, made a little love, and met their friends and families for football parties—basically akin to a north-Mississippi-redneck Heaven, at least according to how some Mississippi State and LSU fans described it.

The cypress door leading into the dean's office opened with a quick creak. Billy walked outside into the hall and closed the door behind him. Billy's red eyes appeared to indicate he might have been crying, but Canon knew how much beer Billy had drunk the night before; plus, the rest of his face was totally devoid of emotion.

A couple of pretty coeds walked by, and Canon said one of them spoke to him, but he just cocked his head and forced a smile to let her know he wasn't interested in talking with anyone at the moment, other than to his friend, Billy Hall.

"Hey, Canonball, I thought you had a chemistry lab at ten," Billy said. "What are you doin' out here?"

"Waiting on you. Screw organic chemistry. It's my ol' man who wants me to be a damn dentist, not me. So what happened in there?" Canon asked. "What'd the dean say?"

"What do you think he said, Canonball?" Billy started walking down the hall toward the water fountain.

"Hell, I don't know. Are you in trouble? *What*?"

"Naw, I'm not in any trouble. None at all. They're not even going to press charges against me for assault." Billy reached the water fountain, leaned over, and drank for several seconds. He leaned back up, wiped his mouth, and faced Canon again.

"Man, that's great! Really! What changed their minds?" Canon said he asked Billy.

"Nothing. They just decided to expel me for a year instead of filing any criminal charges. Nice of 'em, don't you think?"

"What? The jerk was trying to molest Ann Marie! He had it coming to him, Billy!"

Billy started walking toward the glass front doors to leave. "That 'jerk' is also the chancellor's nephew, remember, and currently lying in some bed in the student infirmary in pretty bad shape, so I was told by his uncle."

"Did Dean Montgomery even listen to your side?"

"Sure, he listened." Billy and Canon walked outside the Lyceum and headed for the long flight of concrete steps. Billy lit a Winston. "He even seemed to agree with me at first, until—"

"Until, what?"

"Until Chancellor Wright walked into the office and said he wanted to meet the 'thug' who had almost killed his favorite nephew."

"You've got to be kidding me! This isn't fair, man!"

"Yeah, no shit. But what's fairness ever had to do with anything, Canonball?"

Billy began walking down the steps, which led to the edge of the Grove. Canon stayed on the top step, thinking, he told us, that if he went back inside, he could haul butt down the hall, sprint out the back steps toward the physical sciences building, which was only about fifty yards from the Lyceum, then proffer the standard "barfing" excuse for being so late to his organic chemistry lab.

Billy paused on the bottom concrete step, turned around, and looked up at Canon, who was still standing there, piqued at the injustice just rendered to his best bud from Tupelo. Even from a distance, Canon could see tears in Billy's eyes. "I didn't mean to hurt him like that, Canonball. I swear. I was just trying to protect Ann Marie. I'm sorry. I even prayed for the guy last night, Canonball. I did. I did pray. I *did...*"

"Yeah, I know, Billy. I know. I believe you, man."

Canon continued to watch Billy as he walked dejectedly out onto the green grass of the Grove. He followed him as he languidly wandered around. Then Canon said he saw Billy pull out a tiny slip of pink paper from the pocket of his shirt, and he said Billy stood there reading it, over and over, until he finally crumpled it and threw it on the ground. Billy then vanished into a small covey of hippies, huddled together at the other end of the Grove, stoned as lab rats, and contemplating each other's silver-pierced navels.

Then Canon said he lost Billy.

Canon stood there on the top step of the administration building for several minutes, worried about Billy, and then finally decided, once and for all, he didn't want to go back to Tupelo and practice dentistry with his father and his obnoxious older brother, Everett.

Canon told my parents and me he loathed Everett for always being so mean to him when they were growing up, so there'd probably be an ongoing family feud if he and Everett ever worked together.

And this would be pretty redneck, I thought, *even for Tupelo*.

****

It was probably about the same time Monday morning when I finally awoke in my bedroom and wanted nothing more than to believe Tillman's nocturnal visit had been merely a bad dream. I sat up in bed and stretched, and then I realized my back hurt from helping my folks and those three mover guys carry so many boxes inside. And it certainly didn't help any being awakened at midnight by the nasty nut from across the street. *Darn him. I knew I should've busted his nose when I first had the chance. Then he wouldn't have come back last night*!

I got up out of bed and hobbled over to the window Tillman had climbed through, to check the weather. As I tried to shield my eyes from the sun, I saw my mother outside, standing underneath a huge live oak tree in the middle of our back yard. She was staring at something on the ground. Then she bent over and picked up a baby bird, which had apparently fallen from its nest in the tree. She stood there several seconds, stroking it, and then she started talking to it.

I had always assumed my mother disliked animals, since she never would let us have a dog or even a cat, and I had never seen her show any affection to any sort of critter before, so this perplexed me. Finally, she headed toward the screened back porch, cradling the baby bird in her hands, like she was afraid she might drop it or it might try to escape. She shot a glance toward my room, so I moved away from the window. I didn't want my mother to know I had been spying on her, and I've never told anyone about seeing her and the bird, Monday morning, until now.

****

Something else happened on Monday, our second day in Natchez, I probably should also mention, since Mother got so irate about it.

Dad had gotten up early, and Mother had taken him downtown to his new office on South State Street before I awoke and saw her with the bird. Then she came back home in the station wagon. I learned later Dad had been talking on his phone to Southern Bell Telephone and the Natchez Cable TV Company, to find out when both services would be connected, when President Ed walked into his office and laid the keys to Dad's company car on his desk. Dad said he thanked Ed, but the man had this "weighty look" on his face, and he said something about he and Dad and someone else needing to have a "serious discussion," as soon as possible.

At first, it didn't appear to be any big deal to me. I figured Ed probably wanted to tell my dad to take good care of his old car, or something simple like that. But Ed must have spooked Dad, because Mother told me, much to her chagrin, he had stopped after work at some local bar he had found out about from Jerry Latimer, one of the other insurance agents Dad worked with, and there he drank four Jim-Beam-and-Cokes and smoked several Tareytons before he finally came home crocked, Monday night.

Mother was ready to kill him when he finally got home. And I can't say I blame her, since she had been working hard all day, unpacking the rest of the remaining boxes, toting them out back to the screened porch, and then putting everything in its proper place, including me. She had even found time to go to the A&P, buy a bunch of food and stuff, and then come home to fix beef stroganoff to celebrate Dad's first day on the job. So I wouldn't have faulted her at all if she had hired some North Korean to shoot Dad in his butt again and put herself out of her longsuffering misery.

But more about this later.

****

For me, though, it had been a boring day because the TV cable wasn't hooked up yet, and I had learned, to my *own* chagrin, there were no TV stations in Natchez or anywhere near. The only comfort I took in this was I could use it in rebuke to Tillman's bragging about Natchez being such a "high-class" place. *Yeah, right*, I rehearsed in my mind saying to him. *Natchez doesn't even have a local TV station, you stupid, dung-breath weirdo*!

This really sucked, as far as I was concerned, so I had to spend most of my first whole day in Natchez helping my demanding mother around the house.

First, I helped her unpack the rest of the boxes. Next, we moved all the furniture around and around, and then around some more, until it finally pleased her. Then we had to move it all around some more. I finally told her enough was enough, and I even considered running across the street and begging Tillman to come over to try to help, with his natural flair for arranging things and decorating, but Mother wouldn't have allowed this.

Then I helped her dust and vacuum. I even helped her clean the bathroom, which, she agreed with Tillman, did smell like crap. After this, I got my bedroom in order while Mother mopped the kitchen floor and got all her pots and pans and dishes arranged so she could cook her first home meal, Monday night. When she asked me to go with her to the A&P downtown, though, to help her shop for groceries, I told her, "No," since this was a woman's job. Besides, I was able to convince her I still had a manly chore to do— use my natural flair to hang all our pictures straight, which I finally did.

So that's what I did for the rest of the afternoon. And I thought I did a good job of it, too, except for a couple of places where I had to make *five* holes before I finally got all the pictures straight. But so what? Like I told Tillman, we were just renting the place.

When Mother finally got home with all the groceries she had bought, she surveyed my handiwork, and she didn't tell me to re-hang a single picture. She also didn't tell me, "Good job," but after thirteen years of living with her, I was already accustomed to this.

****

About five-thirty Monday afternoon, Mother was in the kitchen fixing dinner, and I was out in the front yard with my baseball and glove, waiting for Dad to get home. I was just standing there, tossing the ball up in the air and catching it as good as Willie Mays, when I noticed the old stripper staring at me through one of the left parlor windows of her home across the street.

The lace curtains covering both windows were open again. She was standing behind the one she had walked past naked the night before, after she had gone back inside and turned off the front porch light. I almost didn't recognize her at first, since she had clothes on. And her hair looked different. It was wound around the top of her head like a big snake sitting on top of it, instead of hanging long and loose upon her bare shoulders and flapping in the evening breeze.

I stared back at her. She cocked an eye at me, and I cocked an eye at her, and we just stood there, fixated on each other. Then Mother walked up behind me and tapped me on the shoulder. It scared the hell out of me when she did this, since I never heard her approach, and then the bewitching old stripper in the antebellum home across the street quickly closed both lace curtains and walked out of the parlor.

I was about to tell my mother never to do that again, since I almost peed in my pants, but then she said, "The phones are working now. It's for you. It's Billy."

This was the best news I could have possibly heard! I dropped my ball and glove on the ground and ran in the front door like Dad running for his life down a hill in North Korea. I ran straight into the kitchen and grabbed the telephone. It was dangling by its cord from the receiver on the wall. "Hello! Billy, are you still there?" I hollered into it.

"Hey, slow down, buddy boy. I ain't going no

place. I'm still here… So how you liking it down there in Natchez?"

"Man, you're not gonna believe it, Billy! There's this old crazy woman living 'cross the street, and—"

"Yeah, Mother already told me about her. Sounds sorta spooky to me. I'd stay away from there if I were you."

"You sound just like Mother, Billy."

"Well, you know how she is."

"Yeah, she worries too much."

"You know what, Charlie?" Billy laughed. "You sound just like Dad now."

"Gee, thanks. Now we're both screwed up."

"Must be our Presbyterian predestination," Billy said.

"Maybe." As I continued talking to Billy, Mother came into the kitchen from the back porch. She was carrying one of our discarded moving boxes. I noticed it had several holes punched in the top flaps. She gently placed it down on the counter directly beside me, next to the yellow refrigerator. I could tell Mother was pretending she wasn't listening to Billy and me talk, but I knew better.

She had very nosy ears.

So I figured I had better tone it down some. "There's this crazy kid with red hair and bad breath living across the street with her."

"So I heard. What's his name again? Hilburn?"

"No, 'Tillman.' Tillman Dawes. D-A-W—"

"Yeah, that's it, Tillman. Sounds like a weird agent to me."

"For sure. And you know what else, Billy?" I cocked my head a little behind me and noticed Mother out of the corner of my eye, stretching her neck like a goose to try to hear me better. I tried to muffle my mouth with my palm. "He's a real-live Peeping Tom, too."

"Really?"

"Really. He peeped in on Mother and Dad asleep in their bed last night, and then he snuck in through my bedroom window."

"You swear?"

"I do. Well, I guess I sorta let him in."

Mother cleared her throat as soon as I said this. She stirred the pot of beef stroganoff, simmering on the stove.

"But then I made him leave. I probably hurt his feelings, though, 'cause he sounded kinda strange when he left. And you want to know something else?" I checked again to see if Mother was listening. She was. I tried to muffle my mouth even more. "He claims his old home is haunted."

"I can barely hear you. Is Mother listening to us?"

"What do you think? Duh."

"Right. I get you. Try to speak a little louder, though. The dude across the hall has his stereo turned up high. Now, what'd you say about this guy's house? It's *haunted*?"

"It's not a house, it's an antebellum home. You know, one of those old places built by gay guys who hated chicks."

"*What*? Who told you all this crap, Charlie?"

"Tillman. He also said his great-aunt can see and talk to ghosts. She's the one who danced naked on her front porch last night. I just saw her a few minutes ago, too."

"Where?"

"Across the street, inside her home. I was outside in the front yard, pitching to myself. She was staring at me through one of the tall windows in their left front parlor."

"Was she dressed?"

"Yeah, this time. I almost didn't recognize her, at first."

"What'd you do when you saw her?"

"Stared right back at her. I'm not afraid of her. Actually…she's kinda pretty, with her hair up and all her clothes on."

Mother cleared her throat again, much louder this time.

"So what does Pop say about her?"

"He swears she's the best dancer he's ever seen. Claims she reminds him of his Aunt Edna from New Orleans."

"Yeah, I remember her. She got drunk and made me dance with her at Mardi Gras when I was in the seventh grade. Remember?"

"No, not really." Billy paused for a few seconds, so I assumed he probably took a drag from his Winston and a long sip of his Budweiser beer.

"So how's the new house?" Billy finally asked.

"Small and smelly. It's only got one bathroom, and Dad is already hoggin' it. You know, he still claims it takes him so long to go 'cause his butt never has—"

"Yeah, no shit."

"Right, that's what Dad says, too. Get it?"

"Funny. Real funny… You know, you're talking kind of, well, different now, Charlie. How come?"

"Probably 'cause people down here talk different

from us."

"So I've been told. I think this Tillman dude insulted Mother yesterday."

"Wouldn't doubt it a bit. I do feel sorry for him, though. He probably doesn't have many friends, being he's so weird and all. He wants me to start hangin' out with him. Think I should?"

"Do you want to?"

"Don't know yet. I *would* like to meet Tillie, though."

"Who?"

"Tillie, Tillman's great-aunt. The one I just saw."

"The old stripper?"

"Right."

"Well, just don't let her pull an Aunt Edna on you and try to make you dance naked with her." Billy got quiet again, so I assumed he took another hit on his Winston and another sip of Bud. "Anyway, sorry about the house. Guess it'll have to do till Pop can get a better one."

"Yeah, guess so."

"Now, don't talk with Billy too long, Charlie," Mother finally interrupted. "He's calling collect. He probably has to study, and your father will be home soon. Okay?"

"Yes, ma'am, just a little longer." I decided to change the subject. "Mother said you started summer school today."

"It's called 'summer semester,' " Billy advised me. "And I, well…I'm thinking about maybe not going this—"

"You're not going to *school*?" I asked him, much louder than I should have.

That did it. Enough was enough, and it was all my fault. My mother stopped pretending she was deaf. She turned around from the stove and looked me squarely in both eyes. "What did you just say?" she asked me.

"Not so loud," Billy said quickly. "I don't want Mother to know yet. I hope she didn't hear you just say that."

Those were the last words I heard Billy say. Mother stormed over and yanked the phone out of my hand.

"Billy, this is your mother. Did you just tell your brother you're not going to school? I trust I misunderstood him."

Billy probably swallowed his Winston when he heard her ask him this. There was a sickening silence for several seconds. "Oh, hey, Mother. I didn't know you were listening. What I *meant* to tell Charlie is I'm thinking about maybe workin' this summer and not—"

"I asked you a simple question, Billy Hall, and I want a simple answer. Are you or are you not in school this summer?"

"I didn't know she could hear me, Billy!" I shouted out loud so he could hear me. "I promise! I'm sorry…!"

Mother shot a quick glare at me that could have pierced an armored truck, and her eyes told me to shut up. She turned around and spoke into the phone. "Now, you listen to me, Billy. I do not care to discuss this over the phone right before dinner and upset us all, do you hear me? If you're not going to school this summer, then you come straight here, immediately! Do you understand? I expect you down here tomorrow, and this is all I intend to say. Goodbye."

And with that, Mother hung up the phone. I never

got to tell Billy goodbye.

She walked by me back to the stove like I wasn't even standing there and started stirring the pot of stroganoff again. She opened the oven door to check on the rolls like nothing had ever happened. But she was wrong—*way out of line*—and I had no intention of letting Mother get by with treating Billy this way. Or me.

I had this vision of Billy sitting on his bed, stunned by what Mother had just said to him. I could see him throwing his can of beer across the room and it crashing against the wall. I had seen Billy do this before. I never blamed him then, and I didn't blame him Monday afternoon in the kitchen. Somehow, I knew Billy's anger wasn't his fault. I just didn't know why.

Soon, I would learn.

But this time Mother had gone too far. This time she had stirred *my* rage, as well. "I can't believe you just did this!" I shouted toward the back of her head.

"Just did what?" Mother asked, indifferently. She never even turned around to face me.

"You know damn well what! You just ratted on me to my own brother!"

No response. Mother stood there, unmoved. "I've told you before, Charlie—I'll not have you using profanity around me, and I have no idea what you're talking about."

Mother lifted her wooden stirring spoon from the pot so she could taste the gravy. Then she glanced up at the clock over the stove. "I wonder what could be keeping your father so late? There must have been a lot to do on his first day at work, don't you think?"

I couldn't believe her! She could have won an

Academy Award for Most Oblivious Actress in a Family Drama.

"Bring me the garlic salt over there, will you? This gravy is too bland."

I had never been so furious. I wanted to curse her, but I also knew I had lost, again. We *both* had lost. Neither of us had ever learned how to communicate with each other, how to love each other, like Billy and I loved each other.

I reluctantly gave in to Mother's hollow victory. "Now Billy'll never trust me again." I picked up the garlic salt, and I slowly walked over and handed it to her. "Here."

She salted the stroganoff gravy, stirred, and tasted it again. "Yes, much better. Thanks." She turned off the oven, leaned over and got the dinner rolls out, and set the pan on top of the stove. And then, out of the blue, she said, "Well, Charlie, if Billy's going to start lying to us again, I really don't want him confiding in you. I thought you already knew this."

"He *wasn't* lying, Mother. He said he was going to tell you and Dad both when—"

She suddenly turned and glared at me, again. "Oh, really? When, this coming Thanksgiving?"

When I saw the changed expression on her face, I wished she hadn't.

"If he's up there not going to school, spending our money, drinking and carousing with this Ann Marie girl, then he's lying to us. Can't you get this through your simple brain? Quit defending Billy all the time, Charlie. Billy's a liar, pure and simple. That's all there is to it. That's all there ever *has* been to it, and I simply won't tolerate it. Ever again."

Mother turned back around to the stove and turned off the flame on the boiling pot of stroganoff.

She moved it to let it simmer. I was so hurt she was being so cold and mean, I knew I was about to cry. But I refused to give her the satisfaction, so I walked out of the kitchen and into the dining room.

"Oh," she quickly said, "before you leave, Charlie, how about feeding that baby bird in this moving box for me. I stopped by a vet in town this morning, and he gave me some food for it." She pointed with her finger. "It's in the brown paper sack on the dining room table."

I grabbed the bag of birdseed off the dining room table and walked back into the kitchen. I didn't even look at my mother, much less say anything to her. Then I picked up the box off the counter and walked out the kitchen door and onto the back porch. I stared at the box before I set it down on the cold concrete floor.

Poor little bird. Trapped inside my mother's cardboard box, just like Billy and me.

Chapter Five

It was almost seven, and my father wasn't home yet. Mother and I were sitting at the dinner table, she at one end and I at the other, like we were on a blind date and not getting along. As usual, she had on a nice dress and was wearing makeup and lipstick, but I wasn't about to change my dirty clothes, considering all the mean things she had said about Billy that afternoon.

Mother was sitting in her chair, stiff as a corpse, and eating, but she hadn't said a single word in half an hour. The only sound in the house was the loud ticking of Grandpa Hall's Seth Thomas clock, and it was about to drive us both nuts. I could tell Mother was about to explode, and I didn't envy my father when he finally got home.

"I want you to move back to your own chair when your father gets home. You hear me?"

"Yes, ma'am. I hear you."

"Did you see Tillman Dawes again today? Did he come over here?"

"No, ma'am."

"What was he doing out so late last night?"

"Uh, I think I just heard someone drive up." I didn't know she knew. "I'll go see if—"

"You'll do nothing of the sort," she said to me. "Get up now and move your plate back to your own chair so your father can sit there."

"Yes, ma'am."

"Don't forget your tea."

"No, ma'am."

"Here." She stood up from the table and handed me a foil-covered plate, which was next to hers. "Put this in your father's place. I'll not have him think we didn't set him a plate. He's probably exhausted from working so late. I'll warm it for him, if it's cold."

I could tell she didn't really believe this, though, and then I heard the front door slowly open. I breathed a sigh of relief. Dad was finally home.

I was standing at Dad's end of the table, away from the kitchen, and from where I stood I could see him as he crept into the den and then tried to close the door without making a sound. It didn't happen, though, and he cringed when it shut too loudly. He adjusted his tie, carefully hung his navy-blue blazer next to his Yankees cap on the coat stand beside the door, then checked his breath with his left hand. His eyes rolled when he smelled it, so I assumed he was looped. As my dad tried hard to compose himself, I took my seat and didn't dare look over at Mother.

The show was about to begin.

Dad must have finally decided, *Hell, what's the point?* He swaggered through the den and into the dining room like a happy drunk. He walked over and gave Mother a bear hug around the neck, and he kissed her on top of her hair-sprayed head.

You would have thought Mother was being licked by a cow the way she withdrew from his embrace, but I guess Dad's cigarette-and-whiskey breath repulsed her so much it really wasn't worth her pretending.

"The house looks great, Claire!" Dad said, way too

loud. "Thanks for doing all this today. And beef stroganoff, too! Damn, Claire—where'd you find the time to do everything?"

"One would naturally assume," Mother began her assault, without ever looking up from her plate, "you would have at least *called* to say you would be so late."

"Oh? Are the phones working already? I just called the phone company this morning. I didn't expect them to come out so soon."

"You could have at least *tried* to call me, don't you think?"

"You're right, Claire. I'm sorry."

I couldn't tell if Dad was in too good a mood or too inebriated to argue with her. He ambled toward his chair and tussled my hair as he walked behind me. "What's up, sport?" he asked me. Before I could say a word, he sat down in the chair at his end of the table and then suavely tossed his tie back over his shoulder. I thought this was smooth, real smooth.

It was also real stupid. I shot a quick glance toward Mother as she rolled her eyes at him. Dad was undaunted but brazen as he tucked his yellow cotton napkin into his collar and winked at me. "So how's your day been going, sport? Not as hectic as mine, I hope. Cable hooked up yet? I called them this morning, too."

"No, not yet," I told him. I couldn't figure where my dad was getting this "sport" thing from he kept calling me. Then I remembered Billy had mentioned I was starting to talk differently, too, so I figured the native Natchez lingo must be affecting us both. Not Mother, though. Nothing ever seemed to affect her, except Billy. Then I suddenly thought of something. I got up from the table and started to leave.

"Hold on there, sport." Dad leaned across the table and grabbed me by my wrist. "Where you off to so quick?"

"I wanna go see your new car." Dad let go and motioned for me to sit back down.

"Let's save this for later, okay? Plus, it really isn't much to see."

"Thank you, William," Mother remarked. "He's been like this all day." Then she turned her wrath on me. "You aren't going anywhere, young man, until we all finish our dinner. Now, bow your head while your father says grace."

"But I'm almost through, Mother."

"You pray tonight, Claire. I'm really not in the mood," Dad told her.

"So I see," she said. "Yes, this would probably be more appropriate."

To me, this certainly didn't sound like a very Christian thing for Mother to say to Dad, but I figured God probably forgave her for that remark to him because of the pristine, Presbyterian prayer she offered up. Mother proceeded to give thanks for everything and everyone, from the cold carrots to the Cold War. When she finally finished, my father yawned and looked at me.

"It's not even new. It's used."

"What?" I asked him.

"The car—it's a used Buick. We'll go for a ride in it later." He looked across the table at Mother. "It used to be Ed's. He got himself a new one."

"How convenient," Mother replied.

"Well, hell, Claire, it *is* his agency, you know. The

man can do whatever he damn well pleases to."

"Don't you all?" Silence. More silence. Finally, "So do you like your new insurance job, William? I certainly hope so."

"As a matter of fact, yeah…I think it's probably gonna be okay," Dad mumbled back with a mouthful of cold noodles. "They all seem pleasant enough, and Ed seems like a pretty decent fella, so far, but he did mention this morning there's 'something serious' he needs to talk to me about. Can't imagine what it might be, though, can you?"

Dad took a bite of cold beef stroganoff and indicated with his eyes it was good, nonetheless. Mother had this fretful look on her face as Dad rambled on. "There is this one ol' dame down there, though. Heard she's been with the agency since Ed's father started the business. You know the type, Claire, one of those authoritative know-it-alls. The old 'Blue-Blood Broad.' That's what Jerry Latimer, who works there, calls her. Supposedly from some fine old Natchez family which used to have money but doesn't anymore. Now ain't that just a cryin' damn shame," my dad added, as he burped. "Excuse me."

"Maybe she happens to enjoy working, William. Believe it or not, some people do."

"Whatever," he said. "Anyway…yeah, I think the job'll do me, least for the time being." Dad wiped his greasy mouth with the napkin under his chin. "Got any warm rolls, Claire? These darn things are cold as your mother."

" 'For the time being?' Surely, you're not thinking about quitting, already? For God's sakes, William, you just *started* the job! We moved two hundred ninety miles down here to this vile town, and left all our friends and family. Remember?"

"*Your* family, Claire, not mine."

"But *our* friends. And our church."

"Right."

"And I never once complained that the only reason we left Tupelo was because you—"

"Now, did I say I was quitting? Did I? Hell, Claire, Ed loves me! He does. He thinks I'm great! He thinks I'm gonna be a superstar! He said I have 'excellent potential.' Told me so when he hired me; he sure did. Don't you remember me telling you this?"

"No, I don't. I just hope he also believes you can sell insurance and stay at it. Still, I can't fathom how an outsider could possibly sell anything in a closed society like this."

"Aw, Claire, quit your squawking. I could sell Holy Water to a Southern Baptist. And like I heard this preacher on television say one Sunday morning, while y'all were at church, 'Some things just have to be *believed* to be seen.' Made damn good sense to me." Dad looked over at me. "What you think, sport?"

I was tired of being called "sport" by then, but I would never have embarrassed anyone who could be so obnoxious yet so suave and smooth. "Makes sense to me, too, Dad."

"Look, Claire, now we both know I've been drinking, but please don't worry. Okay? Ed runs an old-family, very solid, insurance agency. And all I'm actually doing is servicing existing accounts. They don't even seek new accounts. They don't need to; I promise you. Just trust me this time, okay? Please. It's all I'm asking you. This is our chance, our big escape—

a blessing from God! Can't you just *feel* it?" Dad proclaimed, like some preacher on TV.

"What was this 'something serious' thing you mentioned earlier Ed wants to discuss with you, William?"

"I really don't know. Can't imagine." He took a bite of cold carrots. "But I'm not gonna stay up all night and fret about it. I promise you."

"No, I'm quite sure you won't. You'll leave this up to me to do."

"That's *your* choice, Claire, not mine. Suit yourself. 'Whatever tickles your toes,' like my ol' pop used to say."

"How much money'd you make today, Dad? Have they paid you anything yet?"

Dad looked over at me like he had never heard a stupid question before. "Why do you keep asking me this, Charlie? This is the third time you've asked me in two days."

"Second," I corrected him.

"Right, the second time. Sorry. You're not embarrassed we're living in such a small, inexpensive house, are you?"

"*Renting* a small, inexpensive house," Mother reminded him.

"Oh, no, no. Not at all," I said. "I'd rather live here than in Tillman's big old home across the street, any day. I'm just curious, that's all."

Dad reached over and ruffled my hair again. "Don't be in too big a hurry, Charlie. There're a lot more important things in life than money. Take my word for it."

"Well, I had an interesting phone call from Billy

this afternoon," Mother said, changing the subject.

I had been wondering when she would finally get around to telling him.

"Really? Great!" Dad sounded excited. "How're his classes going?" He took a swallow of melted iced tea.

"This is what's so interesting. They're *not* going."

"What do you mean, 'not going?'"

"I mean they're not going because Billy's not going to them, William. He's not in school this summer."

"*What?* You're not serious. You're kidding me, right?"

"No, I'm quite serious. He didn't have the honesty to tell me when we talked earlier, so he told his younger brother there," she said, pointing her finger accusingly at me.

"I tried to tell her, Dad, but she just wouldn't listen." I looked at my father. "Billy was planning on telling—"

"Don't you contradict me at the dinner table. I've had enough of your impudence for one day, young man!"

"Wait, wait a minute here. Hold on, you two. What do you mean Billy's 'not in school this summer'? I thought he had already registered and started."

"Well, apparently he didn't."

"Then what the hell's he doing up there?"

"Probably drinking and carousing, knowing Billy. That's why I told him to come down here… immediately."

"You don't know this, Mother," I said to her. "Why do you always put Billy down? No wonder I have to defend him all the time."

"Enough! Leave this table and go to your room! I will not have a mere *child* disagreeing with everything I say! Like my mother always said, 'Children should be seen but not heard.' "

"I'm *no*t a child anymore, Mother! Can't you finally get this through your thick skull?"

"How *dare* you insult me and yell at me! If I'd just, just spanked you more, like—"

"Like what, Mother, like you spanked *Billy* all the damn time?"

"Charlie, Charlie…" Dad tried to calm me down.

"*What*?" I turned and shouted at him.

"Please, just please leave the table like your mother's asked, okay? Tell you what…after she and I finish eating, we'll run to town in the car. We'll go to the Burger Chef and get some ice cream. What do ya say, sport?"

"I don't wanna ride in some stupid, used Buick— that's what I say! And I hate Burger Chef ice cream! It…it *sucks*! And quit calling me 'sport,' 'cause I *ain't* one!"

"Charlie Hall! Leave this table *immediately*!" Mother yelled at me.

I stood up from the chair and threw my napkin down on my plate. I stormed from the table and headed straight toward the den.

"Where do you think you're going?" Mother yelled at me, again. "I said for you to go to your room, right this instant!"

"Well, I'm not! So there!"

"Charlie, where are you going?" Dad hollered from the dining room table.

"I'm…I'm goin' over to Tillman's!"

"I told you I didn't want you to ever go over there, young man! Come back here this instant or you're grounded!"

"No!" I yelled back at her as I opened the front door and defiantly walked out. "I'm leaving! I might not *ever* come back!" I slammed the door behind me.

Dad told me later Mother frantically asked him to run out of the house and stop me, but he told her soberly and sincerely, "No, let him be, Claire, just let him be. We need to talk."

Chapter Six

I didn't waste any time. I jumped down the three front steps and hurried across the front yard. It was seven-thirty by then, but there was still daylight left.

I stood at the edge of the street, staring at the Dawes' home for several minutes while I considered whether to go over there. I felt like I was in a theater, watching some horror movie where the hero is staring at a spooky castle on top of a mountain, trying to decide if he should drive up the long, winding road to slay the dreaded monster that lived within.

I remembered my baseball and glove I had dropped when I ran inside earlier to talk to Billy on the telephone. I almost freaked at first when I didn't see them, and I was afraid Tillman or some other Natchez delinquent might have absconded with them. But then I saw them both on the hood of Dad's car. Apparently, he had picked them up when he got home but had left them there in his stupor, so I went over and retrieved them.

I put the leather glove on my left hand and started chunking the ball hard into it. I was pretending the glove was my mother, but then my left palm began to hurt. But I figured this might give me a good excuse to go over to Tillman's. I could knock on their front door and ask him if he wanted to pitch. Sounded sensible to me. After all, what kid didn't like to play pitch?

Even in a weird place like Natchez.

I took a long, deep breath, looked back over my shoulder to make sure my mother wasn't spying out the front window at me, checked to make sure my fly was up, and then I proceeded to leave the sanctum of my front yard.

To me, it was an epiphany, a bold step into the unknown. Freedom, sinful excitement, and a large amount of apprehension swirled into one potentially great adventure. In an instant, I felt totally grown up. I was suddenly an invincible, fearless, nineteen-year-old man about to step off onto not Melrose Avenue toward a haunted mansion across the street, but onto the hills of North Korea to slay the heathen Communists and find and kill the cowards who had shot my dad in the butt. My head was held high—straight up to Heaven—as I bravely, proudly, started to cross over to my destiny—my "hero's journey," as Hank would later call it.

I never saw the Martin's Ice Cream truck, which nearly ran me down. I never even heard its jingle. The hippie-looking teenager who was driving it had to swerve to the left and honk his horn twice to keep from hitting me. So I did what any red-blooded, redneck teenager from Tupelo, Mississippi would have naturally done. I shot the stoned fool the bird and ran across the street and up onto the Dawes' front yard.

I kept running and ran straight up the rickety, wooden steps onto their front porch, out of breath, glove and ball still in hand, and I immediately twisted their doorbell key twice, without even thinking about it. There was a large brass wind chime clanging in the breeze at the left end of their porch, and I was afraid it might have drowned out the sound of the doorbell, so I twisted the old key a third time, just to be sure. I stuck my ear to the etched gold glass on the top part of the door to hear if it was ringing inside.

I also gave a quick glance back over my shoulder to make sure the hippie driver hadn't circled back around the block to whip my butt for flipping him off. Potheads were bad to do this, I reminded myself.

When I looked back around, Tillman had stuck his ugly mug around the faded lace curtain covering the glass to see who was ringing the bell. When he saw it was me, he opened the front door. "Did you think we're deaf in here?" he asked.

"Oh, sorry, Tillman." I pointed toward the other end of the porch. "The wind chimes—they're ringing pretty loud."

Tillman poked his head out the door and looked down the long porch at them. "Oh, yeah," he said. "I hate those damn things. They wake me up sometimes at night. Hank loves them, though. He brought them with him from New Orleans. They're solid, antique brass. Very old and valuable."

I looked at the chimes again and felt intimidated by my obvious lack of knowledge about antiques and such things, so there was no way I was going to ask who this "Hank" person was.

Tillman was staring at my left hand. "So what's with the baseball glove and ball, Hall? You about to go to a game somewhere in town? Well, sorry, but I can't leave now."

"No. I...I just thought you might like to come outside and pitch, that's all."

"'Pitch?' Pitch what?"

"You really don't know what *pitch* means,

Tillman? You swear?"

"I swear a lot, but I don't 'pitch.' Whatever the hell that means."

"Man, I don't believe you. Pitch means to just throw a baseball back and forth to each other and catch it with your… You do have a glove, right?"

"Oh, right, right. Yeah, I knew that; I just forgot. No, we don't do crap like that here in Natchez. It's redneck. Come on in, Hall. You're letting all the ghosts out. Get it?"

"No, I don't."

"Figures."

Tillman opened the door, and I slowly crossed over the threshold into a wild, wonderful world I had never seen the likes of before. The tall front door creaked and closed behind me with the sound of rattling glass. It gave me the chills.

Tillman had called the place an antebellum home the day before, and I had imagined it as a spooky castle or a haunted mansion, but as I stood in the hall and examined the contents of both front parlors, it seemed to me more like an antique store. Both rooms were crammed full of old furniture on old rugs, plus books, paintings, vases, lamps, pottery, dead plants, ticking clocks, mirrors, and, as far as I was concerned, a lot of useless junk. There was a heavy, squalid stench all around, which was a mixture of new cigarette smoke and old mildew, not to mention the smell of Tillman's bad breath as he stood next to me. And there was dust everywhere, like my old bedroom back in Tupelo.

As I stood on a torn, thin rug that ran the length of the long front hall and tried to take it all in, my first thought was, *Where'd they get all this old stuff from?*

This was soon followed by an un-Christian but enticing thought, *It'd probably kill my mother if she had to dust it all.*

There was a steep staircase at the far end of the hall with stained red carpet running all the way to the top. It reminded me of the scene in *Gone With the Wind* where Rhett carries Scarlet all the way to the top of the stairs and eventually, I always assumed, throws her onto a bed. But there was no way I would have gone up all those stairs, sex or no sex.

The next thing which caught my attention, and there was no way to miss it, was a full-size medieval knight in armor standing guard at the bottom of the stairs, holding a large silver-and-brass sword in its hands. I naturally assumed the thing was stationed there to thwart normal kids, like me, from venturing upstairs. It definitely worked.

I left Tillman standing at the front door and started slowly walking down the long hall, gawking at everything and shaking my head in amazement. I heard Tillman say something about not tripping on the runner, but I didn't see anyone running around in there.

There were two connecting parlors on both sides of the hall. Three of the rooms were wide open, so I walked inside and examined them all, one by jam-packed one. I wanted to ask Tillman why they didn't sell some of their things I saw all around me, because there was no way they could possibly have needed or used them all; also, there was no telling how much money they could have gotten for them. But I would later learn Natchez "blue-bloods" loved old stuff. They even had a word for it: "heirlooms," and they never sold any of them, even when they *did* need the money.

It didn't make any sense to me, but I figured this was what Dad meant when he told me earlier there were some things in life more important than money.

I finally came to the far parlor on the right, next to the staircase, and I noticed both its tall, golden oak doors were slid together and tightly shut. This was fine with me because, unless you were one of the Three Stooges, no one in his right mind would have dared to open them.

"If you'd like the grand tour," Tillman said from the front end of the hall, "it'll cost you three bucks. That's what all the Yankee tourists used to pay when Great-Uncle Oliver was alive."

"Man, where'd y'all get all this old stuff, Tillman?" I looked up the hall at his skinny self, still standing by the front door. "This place looks like an antique store, or a museum!"

"You ain't seen nothing yet, Hall," he said back to me. "Wait till we go upstairs and I show you the four bedrooms and what all's in the attic. You're really going to freak, then!"

"Uh, that's okay, Tillman." I looked over my shoulder and tried to see all the way up those stairs. "Not tonight. Maybe some other time, during the day." I pointed my finger at the closed parlor doors directly in front of me. "What's in this room here?" Then I foolishly tried to pry them apart.

"No, no!" Tillman screamed like a frightened girl watching a zombie movie. "Don't dare open them!" He sprinted down the hall, almost tripping on the runner rug, and grabbed me by my right arm. He was nearly out of breath when he said, "No! You can't go in there, Hall. Not ever! It's totally off limits to unbelievers."

"I'm a believer. I'm Presbyterian," I informed him.

"You don't understand, Hall. You can't even *begin* to imagine what's going on inside there, even as we speak! Nobody's allowed in there unless they're invited in by Hank or Tillie. Not even *me!*"

"Why? What's the big deal? What's in there, ghosts?"

"You don't know what you're asking, Hall, you really don't." Tillman finally caught his cigarette breath.

"Then why'd you crawl in my window last night and try to drag me out of bed to come over here? Huh?"

"What are you talking about? I didn't crawl in your window last night. You must have been dreaming."

"You did so! About twelve o'clock last night! I wasn't dreaming. I was wide awake, and I saw you! You're a liar!"

"Am not!"

"Are too! I oughta bust your nose right here!"

"I know karate, Hall! I wouldn't try that if I—"

"Shut up, Tillman. Be quiet..." I stared at the parlor doors.

"Why?"

"Shhh. I just heard something in there... I hear voices."

"I don't hear anything."

"You're lying, Tillman. Of course you do. Listen, I can hear people talking inside there. Who all's in this room?"

"Nobody."

"Liar, liar, pants on fire!"

Tillman looked down at the baseball cupped in the glove in my left hand. "Listen, Sherlock Holmes, why don't we just go outside before it gets dark and pitch your damn ball."

"Be quiet, Tillman!" I leaned forward and put my left ear to the door. "I can hear this woman in there. She's mumbling something." I tried hard to listen closely. "And some man's in there with her, crying and moaning, like he just lost his—"

The two parlor doors suddenly flew apart! I dropped the baseball on the floor and almost wet all over myself when I saw who or what I thought was the devil himself, standing before me.

He was short, bald, and grubby, with a big belly which smothered his belt. He looked to be about sixty-five, to me. He had a black patch over his left eye, a cigarette in his right hand, and he was dressed like a Catholic priest. I panicked and started to run for my young, Protestant life.

The portly priest grabbed me by my left arm and knocked the glove out of my hand.

"Now, just hold on there, tyro. Not so fast. I was wondering who this was, causing all this damn ruckus out here in the hall."

"I tried to warn him, Hank! I swear I did! He's a redneck from Tupelo and just doesn't know any better," Tillman shouted.

The one-eyed priest named Hank put his tobacco-stained index finger to his lips and motioned for Tillman to stop all his squawking. "No harm done, my young, fickle friend. Nothing to fret about," Hank told Tillman. Then he focused his one gray eye on me. "They're still in a trance. Fortunately for you both, they aren't aware you're here. Have a look, son…"

I peeked around Father Hank's bulging belly and

couldn't believe my eyes. On the far side of the parlor, next to the fireplace, the mysterious woman I saw at the window, who I knew had to be Tillman's Great-Aunt Tillie, was seated at a card table holding hands with a younger man dressed in a coat and tie, sitting across from her. Tillie was dressed like Dracula's wife, and she had this purple scarf on top of her head, wrapped all around it, like she was fixing to take a shower. There was a lit candle on one side of their arms and a crystal ball as big as a grapefruit on the other. To me, it looked like a scene from some cheap horror movie.

"What are they doing over there?" I asked both Tillman and Hank. "Why are they holding hands?"

"Silence," Hank admonished me. "They're communing. We mustn't disturb the present moment."

"'Communing?'" I asked, curiously.

"Yeah, Hall, communing…with ghosts. Don't you know *anything*? What'd you think they're doing in there, about to smooch?" Tillman said, sarcastically.

"Don't be haughty, Tillman. It's very crude manners," said Hank. "And, technically speaking, they're called 'spirits.' "

"Told you, Tillman."

"Same thing." Tillman stuck out his nasty tongue at me.

"But I don't understand," I said. "How do you 'commune' or whatever with a spirit, if it's already—"

Before I could finish my question, the guy with the tie jumped up from the card table and almost knocked the crystal ball and candle over. Tillie grabbed them both before they fell to the old rug on the brown painted floor.

"Oh, my God!" the guy started shouting. "Oh, my

God! I see her; I see her! It's really her! Jan, Jan…! It's me!'"

Confused, I searched the dimly lit parlor with my eyes for this Jan woman, but I couldn't see her anywhere. Hank closed his right eye and shook his bald head for me to stop doing this.

"Jan, Jan!" he cried. "It's me, Lou, your ex-lover! Don't you recognize me? I want you, Jan—I need you…!" Then Tillie started whistling "He's Got the Whole World in His Hands." The man dropped to the floor on his knees, covered his face with his hands, and began to weep loudly. "She's gone, she's gone, she's gone," he kept wailing.

"Excuse me, lads," Hank said to Tillman and me, "but I must go help console our poor, grieving client. Alas, Jan's spirit has retreated for the evening."

Hank wallowed over to this Lou fellow, who was on his knees, still weeping, and helped him get up. I heard someone sniffling and looked over at Tillman. I couldn't believe it, but he had tears in his eyes. At first, I thought he was faking it, but as I stared at Tillman for a few seconds, his tears looked real to me. I started to ask Tillman if he and this Lou guy were related, but I figured he'd probably explain later. Besides, I was mainly interested in what was going on inside the parlor.

Hank put both his huge hands on top of Lou's shoulders. "Your ex-lover, Jan, has gone back now, Mr. Milam. Crossed forever the 'Great Divide.' Look for her…no more."

"You, you mean Mrs. Dawes can't bring her back to me? I'll, I'll never see her again?"

"Not tonight, sir." Hank told him. "Not tonight.

Maybe this Friday—say, about ten?"

"Please, please, I beg you! You must! Tonight!"

"I'm afraid this is impossible," Hank said.

Tillie seemed to awaken from her trance, or whatever it was she was in. She opened her eyes and said in an eerie-sounding voice, "Mr. Milam, Mr. Milam…" Her arms were still outstretched on the card table, her hands clasped together. "Your dearly departed ex-lover, Jan, left me with one final message to deliver to you."

"What? For Christ's sakes, Madam Dawes—what?"

"Go home to your pregnant wife and kids. Jan is peaceful and happy now, and she desires the same for you," Tillie told him.

With this, Hank threw his arms up in the air, more like a Pentecostal preacher than a Catholic priest, looked up at the twelve-foot-high ceiling, and shouted, "The madam has spoken—Hallelujah! Hallelujah!"

"Yes, it is finished," Tillie added. She blew out the candle, stood up from the coffee table, stretched her long, thin arms out in front of her, locked her fingers together, and cracked her knuckles. Then she looked over at Hank and Lou and said in a normal voice, "Whew. Well, I don't know about you two, but I could use a drink."

Hank agreed. "My thoughts exactly, Mrs. Dawes. Coming right up." Hank looked at Lou, who had this baffled look on his face. "How about you, my good sir?" he asked. "What'll it be? Vodka, I hope. It's all we have."

"No, no, I don't like vodka. I mean, I don't indulge. I never have."

"You're kidding me. Hell, man, this is Natchez!" Hank slapped Lou's back. "*Everyone* drinks here!"

"No, seriously. It's against my religion to drink."

"Interesting." Hank rubbed his unshaven chin and said. "Drinking's against your so-called 'religion,' but philandering's not. Never heard such hypocritical balderdash before."

Hank turned to Tillman and me, still standing in the open parlor doors. "Now, *entrez*, Master Tillman…*entrez*!" he exclaimed. "And just who might your compadre there be? I don't believe we've yet been formally introduced."

Tillman walked into the room, but I stayed put at the door, just in case I decided to make a run for the front door.

Tillie noticed me standing there, looking like I had just seen a ghost, and pointed at me from across the room. "Hey, I know you," she said. "You're the new kid from across the street. You were in your front yard this afternoon, staring at me through my window. Why? I saw you."

I started to tell her she was the one who was staring at me, but I was afraid she might turn me into a toad, or perhaps a stray cat.

Tillie walked across the room and extended her wrinkled hand to me like she was running for a political office. "I'm Sharon Tillman Dawes. Very happy to finally meet you, son."

I shook her hand. "Hello, I'm Charlie. Charlie Hall. Pleased to meet you, ma'am."

Tillie looked over at Hank and smiled. "Confident young chap, wouldn't you agree so, Father Ishee?"

"I do, Mrs. Dawes. I do, indeed. I wouldn't dare

not to."

"Be careful," Tillman piped up. "He's not one of us. He's from north Mississippi…Tupelo!"

Tillie raised both eyebrows, and Hank coughed. Lou looked at me warily, like he had never seen a north Mississippi redneck before.

I glared over at Tillman. I wanted to slug him.

"He is most welcome, nonetheless. I have a very good feeling about this young man," Tillie said to everyone present.

"You're Tillman's great-aunt, aren't you, Mrs. Dawes? He told me all about you when we moved down here yesterday."

"Well, more or less," she said, "but please, Charlie, call me 'Tillie.' I insist."

"Well, yes, ma'am. Sure, if you say so."

Hank walked across the room and joined us. He leaned over to me and whispered with breath as bad as Tillman's, "She says so, and if I were you, tyro, I'd do what Tillie says."

"What's a 'tyro'? Why are you calling me this?"

Hank straightened back up and didn't answer me. Tillie motioned with her head to Hank, and he got the message. Hank walked over to a tattered, green sofa in the center of the room, under a dusty crystal chandelier, reached under one of the old cushions, and retrieved a half pint of vodka. He proudly held it up toward the light and exclaimed, "Aha, 'foodka'!"

Tillie looked over at Lou, who was standing there, forlornly. "His Russian stinks, don't you think so, Mr. Milam?"

"Uh, yeah, I guess so," Lou mumbled. He looked at his watch. "Well, I guess I had better be going now.

Getting kind of late. Big day at the bank tomorrow. Tuesday's our—"

"So soon?" Tillie asked. "We haven't even toasted the session yet. It's traditional."

"I'm sorry, Mrs. Dawes. Really. It's my kids. They're young and home alone. Sonja's out with a friend tonight."

"Yes," Tillie responded, "you *do* need to be going then. You shouldn't have left them alone at home. Shame on you, Mr. Milam."

Lou reached in his back pocket for his wallet. "So…how much do I owe you for tonight's session?"

Tillie glanced over at Hank, who was just finishing a big swig of vodka, and winked at him. Hank wiped his mouth on the sleeve of his priest's jacket, screwed the blue bottle cap back on, and winked back at her. Then Tillie said to Lou, "Well, let's just see, now. Tonight was kind of *special*, wouldn't you agree, Mr. Milam?"

"*How* special?" Lou asked, cautiously.

Hank walked over to Lou, opened the bottle, took another sip, then put his hand on Lou's shoulder. "*Damn* special, my son. Hell, a *miracle* happened in here tonight!"

"A 'miracle' sounds expensive, to me." Lou raised his eyebrows.

"Well, Lou, take it from an ex-priest: God's miracles don't come cheap."

"No, no, I certainly can't argue with that," said Lou.

Tillie clenched her fists, gritted her teeth, walked up to Hank, and got right in his face.

"Fifty," she told him flatly.

"Sixty," Hank quickly said back.

"Seventy."

"Eighty."

"Seventy-five," Tillie told him, two eyeballs to one eyeball.

"Eighty, Madam Dawes. I say eighty, damn it!" Hank railed with his arms folded. "I insist!"

"Very well, Father Ishee, have it your way." She turned and spoke to Lou. "Seventy-five dollars it is, Mr. Milam."

"Seventy-five dollars? Isn't this a bit steep, even for a miracle?" Lou asked.

"Hey, didn't you hear me over here negotiating with him for you?" Tillie replied.

"Well…okay. Whatever." Lou put his wallet back into his pocket and reached for his checkbook and pen inside his coat. "Will you take a check? I'm a little short on cash tonight."

Tillie turned back around to Hank. "Father Ishee, will the spirits accept Mr. Milam's check?"

"Don't you mean, Mrs. Dawes," Hank replied, "will they accept Mr. Milam's *gift*? Why, yes, dear lady, of course, they will; of course, they will!" Then Hank looked at Lou. "They first want to know if it's good, though."

"Why, certainly it's good, Father Ishee!" Lou protested. "I work for a damn *bank*, for Christ's sakes!"

"Just wanted to make sure, my son. Spirits detest bad checks, you know. Makes them mad as hell, in fact."

"Well, I certainly don't want to do that, I assure you."

Tillie took the bottle of vodka from Hank's hand

and took a big swallow. "Good idea, Mr. Milam." She handed the bottle back to Hank.

Lou began to write. "Who should I make this out to?"

"Me," Tillie said. The doorbell rang. Tillie looked at Tillman and me. "Tillman, go answer the front door. See who this might be, please."

"I bet it's my mother," I said. "She's probably come to get me and take me home."

"Oh? Well, in this case, then, I better go answer it." Tillie proceeded to walk out of the parlor. "Tillman, tell Mr. Milam how to spell 'Dawes.' "

I followed Tillie out of the parlor and stood outside the two sliding doors as I watched her gracefully sashay up the hall toward the front door. Her hands were extended on both sides like she was modeling on a stage walk, dressed like a witch.

The doorbell rang again, and Tillie almost tripped on a torn part of the hall rug when one of her black high-heeled shoes got caught in it. "Damn this old runner!" Tillie said, not knowing I could hear her. She hollered toward the front door. "I'm coming, damn it, I'm coming! Keep your panties on…"

Tillie flipped on the front porch light and opened the door. A short and frail woman, much older than Tillie, wearing more jewelry than a pawn shop has in it, and smoking a long cigarette in an ivory holder, was standing outside the door and rearranging her blue-gray hair.

"Why, Mrs. Kowalski!" Tillie exclaimed. "I, I didn't realize it was you."

"I do hope I'm not too early, Madam Dawes." The older lady said in a refined but raspy voice. She turned around and spoke to someone standing behind her. "Perhaps, though, this pretty young lady here might—"

"No, no, not at all." I quickly stepped behind the parlor doors so Tillie wouldn't know I had been spying on her. Tillie turned and hollered down the hall, obviously hoping Hank would hear her, "In fact, our last session *just finished*! *Just…now…finished*!"

Apparently, Hank did. When I looked into the parlor, Hank was in the rear of the room, opening a door for Lou that led to some steps going outside. As Lou left, Hank closed the door and locked it. Then he smiled at me. "Clients prefer not to see each other. I'm sure you understand. Sort of like Southern Baptists do when they see each other in a liquor store."

"Yeah," Tillman added, "and they're all kin, too. At least here in Natchez they are."

I stuck my head outside the doors again and peered up the long hall at Tillie. She was pulling a pocket watch on a gold chain from one of the pockets of her black lace dress. She popped open the lid, then slipped the watch back inside her dress. "You are exactly on time, Mrs. Kowalski," Tillie told her. "Please, come in. We mustn't keep Morris waiting."

Mrs. Kowalski cleared her smoke-damaged, old throat. "As I was about to say, Madam Dawes…" Mrs. Kowalski turned around to the person standing behind her. "Perhaps this lady has a much more pressing engagement, though. Morris can wait."

Tillie peeked around Mrs. Kowalski, and I almost fainted when the old lady with the cigarette holder stepped aside. My mother was standing behind her, her arms folded, stone-faced, and impatiently tapping her right shoe on the porch.

Mother stepped up, thanked Mrs. Kowalski, and attempted a smile that just didn't work.

"Excuse me for interrupting, Mrs. Dawes, but I'm looking for my thirteen-year-old son. I presume he is here?"

"Oh," Tillie said, "you must be Charlie's mother? Yes, he's here. He said it might be you at the door. Do come in, Mrs. Hall, and I'll go tell—"

"No. Just please tell him to come back home, *immediately*. Thank you."

With this, my mother turned around, without even saying "good night," and headed toward the front steps. Both Tillie and Mrs. Kowalski watched as she walked down the steps and proceeded toward the front yard.

"Well!" Mrs. Kowalski said. "That was certainly rude."

"*Bitch*," Tillie added.

"Yes, isn't she, though," Mrs. Kowalski agreed as she took a drag from her cigarette holder. "Must be a Yankee."

"No, far worse—north Mississippi. Tupelo."

"Oh, my. No wonder, then."

"In any event, do come in, Mrs. Kowalski. Please."

The old, worn-out widow walked inside. "Thank you, Madam Dawes," she said, respectfully. "You are most kind."

"Would you wait here a moment, please? I'll be right back. I just need to make sure the parlor is ready for you."

Tillie turned around, and I jerked my head back behind the doors again. I could hear her walking quickly down the hall, so I hurried over and sat down next to Tillman on the sofa. Hank was standing on one leg, like a pink flamingo, trying to impress Tillman by balancing a nearly empty vodka bottle on the top of his bald head. "Now, watch very closely, Tillman. I learned this little trick back in seminary school…"

Tillie marched into the parlor and barked at Hank, "Cut the crap, *padre*! It's Mrs. Kowalski for her eight-thirty!"

The half-pint vodka bottle slid down Hank's head, but he caught it before it hit the floor. "Ta-da!" Hank gleamed.

"Better be going, Charlie," Tillie said, looking at me. "That was your mama at the door, too, and she's pissed you're over here."

I looked at Tillman. "What'd I tell you, huh? I've really blown it, now. I better get my butt back over there before Mother calls the law on me."

Hank bent over and winked his eye at me. "Don't worry, tyro. I know all the cops in town. Hell, the chief of police and I are best friends!"

"Really?" I asked Hank. I was impressed.

"Don't believe a word Hank says tonight," Tillman told me. "It's just the cheap vodka talking. He's hammered—has been since six."

"This is a lie, Tillman Dawes!" Hank roared. "I've been hammered since five!"

I stood up and started to leave. Tillman sat there and scratched himself in a place where you shouldn't scratch yourself in the presence of other people.

"You, too, Tillman. Scoot! You know Mrs. Kowalski doesn't like for you to watch," Tillie told him.

"I won't start crying this time, Tillie. I swear it. I like Morris. He's a funny old Jew."

"Yes, he is, and Morris likes you, too. But *Mrs.* Kowalski doesn't, and she's the one who's paying. So scram."

"Vamoose, boy, vamoose," Hank ordered, jerking Tillman up by his arm from the sofa.

Before I left, I looked at Hank. "What's a 'tyro,' Father Ishee? Why did you call me that tonight? I've never heard this word before."

"Not surprising. Most folks haven't. It's an old word I used to teach my students which simply means 'a beginner in learning.' And tonight, my new young tyro, we shall begin your journey. So *adieu…adieu…*"

"This is why I hate vodka. Fries your brain cells," Tillman whispered to me again as we walked toward the open parlor doors.

"Now I believe you," I said, as I picked up my baseball and glove, lying near the doors.

Tillman and I walked out of the parlor and headed up the hall. Mrs. Kowalski was still standing by the front door, holding another long cigarette in her white-gloved right hand.

"Tillman, please tell Mrs. Kowalski she can come on back now!" Tillie hollered from inside the parlor.

We walked up the hall to the front door. Mrs. Kowalski snuffed out her cigarette in a blue ashtray on the table next to the door. Then she put her cigarette holder inside her old purse.

"They're ready for you now, Mrs. Kowalski. Please tell Mr. Morris hello for me."

She nodded at Tillman. "Thank you, Tillman. I shall." Mrs. Kowalski smiled politely at us both, and then she shuffled her old legs toward the far parlor at the right end of the long hall.

Tillman and I opened the door and walked out onto the front porch. It was dark by then, and the crickets seemed to be chirping much louder than they did in Tupelo. I reminded myself to tell Billy even crickets talked differently in Natchez.

"Man, she's gonna kill me," I told Tillman.

"Who, your mom?"

"Yeah. She ordered me not to ever come over here."

"Why?" he asked me.

"Why? Because a houseful of *crazies* live here! Tillman, my folks and I saw Tillie dancing naked out here last night."

"So? She only dances when there's a full moon out."

"Well, she oughta do it inside so nobody will see her."

"Aunt Tillie says she likes to be seen. She used to be a stripper down in New Orleans. Made big bucks at it, too."

"You're just lying again, Tillman. I hate it when you lie to me."

"No, I swear! That's where she met Hank the Yank."

"*Hank the Yank?*"

"Right. Hank's a Yankee. From Chicago. Get it?"

"Oh, yeah. I see. I thought he talked kinda different, even for Natchez. So what's his story? Man, if he ain't one strange bird, I don't know who is. Is he really a priest?"

"He used to be. Well, not a *real* priest. He said he was a 'Jesuit,' or something like that. He used to teach at some Catholic prep school down in New Orleans, for years. I think he said he taught English lit and philosophy."

"My dad's from New Orleans." I walked down the front steps as Tillman followed me. "So how'd he and your Great-Aunt Tillie hook up?"

"Well, after Great-Uncle Oliver finally died, Aunt Tillie said to hell with Natchez and moved down to New Orleans. This was a long time ago, when she was young. She was beautiful and sexy back then. I've seen lots of pictures of her. Anyway, the only job Tillie could find there was stripping at some sleazy joint on Bourbon Street. 'The Ritz Tits,' I think it was called."

"My dad's from New Orleans."

"Right, Hall. I heard you the first time. Duh."

We ambled across the front yard toward Melrose Avenue. Tillman slapped a mosquito on the back of his neck. "Damn these bugs!"

"You mean Tillie made enough money stripping to buy this antebellum home and all the old stuff inside there?" I glanced back over my shoulder, as I asked.

"No, Hall, of course not. This place had been in Uncle Oliver's family for generations. He left it to her after he passed away."

"Oh, cool. They didn't have any kids, huh?"

"Nah. I overheard Tillie confess to Hank once that fat Uncle Oliver never liked to do it much. But Aunt Tillie's always loved kids. So she adopted me."

"After your folks were killed, right?"

"Right."

"This sure was Christian of her."

"Yeah, that's what Hank always says, too." Tillman smiled and showed his nasty teeth. We stopped at the edge of the street. "After she got too old and wrinkled to strip anymore, she moved back up here to her old home," he added.

"So how'd she and Hank hook up?"

"Aunt Tillie told me Hank, who was Father Ishee then, used to come down to the French Quarter and watch her strip every Friday night after school was out. He and some other priest friend of his. They'd dress up like tourists, get all liquored up, take a cable car over to Canal, and then head across to Bourbon Street to the Ritz Tits. Tillie told me she never knew where Hank got all the money from—he was one of her biggest tippers. Then she said she figured it out after Hank finally got caught and the Jesuits booted him out."

"For going to a strip club?"

"Nah, that really wasn't any big deal. He got the axe 'cause he'd been stealing money from his school's Korean Missions Fund. That's where he got all the dough to tip her."

"My dad hates North Koreans. They shot him in the butt when he was running for his life down a hill over there."

"Bummer. It must be hard for him to sit down on a hard commode seat and crap, huh?"

"No shit, get it?"

"Hey, that was good, Hall—really good! You know, you just might make it here in Natchez after all."

"So how'd Hank get up here to Natchez with Tillie?" I asked him.

"Tillie said she sorta felt responsible, you know, for helping corrupt Hank. So after the Catholic Church excommunicated him, Tillie took him in. Then they eventually moved up here."

"That's a wild story, Tillman. You aren't just

making up all this bull, are you?"

"It's *not* bull; it's true! Ask Hank. Ask Tillie, too."

"I just might."

"Then do it, Perry Mason!"

I threw the ball into my glove several times while I thought. "Let me ask you something else, Tillman. Is Tillie some sort of witch or something?"

"Hell, no, she's not a damn witch! She's a medium."

"A medium what?" My left palm hurt again, so I stopped pitching to myself.

"A 'medium,' Hall. She conjures up ghosts, spirits."

"Oh… So that's what they were doing behind those big doors. This Lou guy thought he was seeing a spirit, right?"

"No, wrong, Hall. He didn't just *think* he saw her—he *did* see her. Didn't you hear him screaming his fool head off in the séance parlor?"

"Yeah, but I just figured he was probably stoned or something."

"Like I tried to tell you last night, Hall, it—"

"Wait a minute, Tillman. You told me you didn't come—"

"Sorry. I meant like I tried to tell you *yesterday afternoon*, it really is true. Aunt Tillie can make spirits appear. I've seen 'em. She has spirit friends, too. They do things for her."

"Yeah, right, Tillman… Like what?"

"Like grant requests for her. Other people, too."

"What kind of requests?"

"Whatever you want."

"That's just a bunch of bunk, Tillman. People

who've died can't do things for people who're still living. I'm goin' home. Goodnight!" I started to run across the street, dreading what awaited me, though, after I walked into our house.

Just as I stepped onto Melrose Avenue, Tillman spoke in the same, strange voice he had used the previous night, right before he left my room. "Jesus died, Charlie, and He does things for people all the time. Don't you believe this?"

His different-sounding voice sent chills down my spine. I was too frightened by how Tillman said this, and too ashamed I had forgotten it, to turn around and face him, even in the dark.

This time, I looked both ways before I darted across the street. I stopped at the edge of our yard, thought for a few seconds, then turned around. I could barely see him. "Hey, Tillman," I yelled over to him, "if you're telling the truth, then tell your Great-Aunt Tillie to ask her spirit friends to do something for me!"

"You have to give them a gift first!" Tillman yelled back.

"What kind of gift?"

"Depends!"

"On what?"

"On what you want, Hall. Duh!"

It didn't take me long to think. "I…I want everyone at my new school next year to like me, and I want to make all A's, without ever studying! So what kind of gift d'you think this'll take?"

"I don't know! I'll hafta ask Hank! He's in charge of the gifts department! Meet me back here later at twelve, and I'll let you know! Oh, and Hall…!"

"What?"

"This time, don't be late!"

I turned and hurried up the sidewalk to our house. Like Dad had done earlier, I opened the front door and tried to close it slowly, gently…soft as a poot in church. But there she was, standing watch in the den, like the knight in rusted armor at the foot of the Dawes' stairs.

"I specifically told you to never go over there. You're grounded, effective immediately."

"But, Mother, I…I just—"

"Don't lie to me. You deliberately disobeyed me after I ordered you to go—"

"What was I supposed to do, Mother? Sit here all night and listen to y'all pretend like you love each other?"

"I don't intend to argue with you anymore, Charlie Hall. Go to your room like I told you to before you left this house."

"What did I do so wrong, Mother? Please, tell me! What are you so damn afraid of?"

She drew back her hand to slap my face, but I ran past her through the den, down the hall, and into my bedroom. I slammed the door behind me and hardly even noticed my dad, passed out cold on the sofa and snoring like a hibernating bear.

When I finally got through crying and cussing, I could hear her in the kitchen through my bedroom wall, talking loudly, like she was trying to communicate with someone who couldn't hear very well. Or some*thing* that couldn't hear at all.

"How's my little baby doing in there?" I heard her say. "Mama's going to take good care of you. Don't you worry, now… Well, I was right. Charlie was over there. He finally came home, though. And now he's grounded, just as Mother and I agreed he should be."

Mother must have brought the moving box back into the kitchen from the back porch, where I had taken it. She was talking to the baby bird inside it, like it was her child or something.

"And wouldn't you just know it? William never said one word to him," she told the bird. "Yes, he's still passed out on the sofa. Yes, I know he's never going to change. I'm worried about Charlie, though. Mother said I have to get a better handle on Charlie or else I might lose him too, like she said I lost Billy."

I didn't hear anything more for several seconds, so I assumed she had probably caught the baby bird and had taken it out of the box to stroke its feathers. After all, I had already seen Mother do this in our back yard, that morning.

Then I heard her tell it, "Billy's coming down here to Natchez tomorrow. I told him he belongs here, at home with us. Not up there with that Ann Marie tramp. Just like my mother and I agreed. This *was* the correct thing to do, wasn't it? Wasn't it...?"

That baby bird was smarter than I thought. I never heard it agree with Mother.

Chapter Seven

Based on what Ann Marie told us later, I can only imagine the terrible day Billy must have had.

About the same time Monday evening, Ann Marie and Billy were sitting at a table in Cangemi's, drinking beer and eating pizza. Ann Marie said the place was packed—first night after classes—and that Billy had been waiting ten minutes for a third beer, something which would have normally perturbed him. But Billy was unconcerned, distant, and sober, she added.

Finally, one of the waitresses—Ann Marie knew her from their spring semester Spanish class—walked up to their table and brought Billy his Budweiser. "Thanks," Billy told her.

"Ann Marie," the waitress asked, "what about you?"

"No. Thanks. I'm fine." Then she asked her former classmate, "Are you taking any courses this summer, Beth?"

"No," Beth said, "just working, trying to make enough money to pay for next fall. Daddy got laid off in March from the mill in Grenada. We don't know how long the shutdown will last."

"I'm so sorry to hear this," Ann Marie said she told Beth.

"Thanks," Beth replied. "Please keep our family in your prayers, will you? It's kind of tough, right now."

Ann Marie took Beth's hand. "I will. I promise, Beth. Don't worry, God will see y'all through this. He always does."

"I know this, and I do believe it, but sometimes I forget." Beth had tears in her eyes. "Thanks, Ann Marie. I better get back. It's crazy in here tonight. I'll check on y'all later."

"Good luck, Beth." Ann Marie looked at Billy, who had only been half-heartedly listening to them. "The poor girl," Ann Marie said. "I feel sorry for her, don't you, Billy? She's such a sweet girl and so pretty. I wish I could help her."

"Yeah, me too. I can definitely relate. So how about keeping me in your prayers, too? I could use some right now."

"I pray for you every day, Billy. You know that."

Billy took a sip of his Bud. "Well, I hate to tell you this, but I don't think God was listening very close this morning."

"You know better than this. You know that's not true."

Billy didn't reply, Ann Marie told us. She said he quickly changed the subject. "How's your pizza? I really like this new place. Glad it finally opened. The Rebel Hut was getting old. Food there just wasn't too good anymore."

"Yes, I agree. Mine's excellent," she said. Ann Marie told us she really wasn't interested in making small talk, but she knew better than to bring up the subject of what had happened before Billy was ready to discuss it. She said she knew him too well and loved him too much to ever do this, "prematurely." Ann Marie sat thinking for a while.

They ate in silence for a few minutes. Billy had eaten most of his large sausage, beef, and cheese pizza. Ann Marie had eaten only half of her medium pepperoni. Billy took a long swig of his third Bud. Ann Marie was still sipping on her first bottle of Miller High Life.

More long silence. Ann Marie sat there as she watched Billy continue to eat and drink beer. When Billy had finally finished, he belched twice, and waved his hand for Beth to bring him his fourth brew. Ann Marie decided she had been patient for long enough. Love or no love, she said, it was time to talk.

She reached across the small table and put Billy's hand between hers. "Billy, don't you think we need to discuss what happened today?"

"Why? What's there to discuss? It is what it is." Billy finally caught Beth's attention as she was leaving a table of four Sigma Chis, Ann Marie claimed, sitting next to the bar.

"I don't agree with this. I think things always happen for a reason. We just have to trust in God."

"C'mon, Ann Marie, you're starting to sound like my mother. I really don't want to hear another lecture on religion, like you just gave that Beth girl."

"I'm not talking about 'religion,' Billy. I'm talking about simple faith, believing, trusting God to handle this."

"Yeah, well, I tried trusting God, once. All it did was make me cry. My prayers weren't exactly answered. It hurt. Really bad."

"Yes, I know. It sometimes does."

"Well, I'm sorry and all, but I'm really not interested in getting hurt again. If you wanna pray—

hey, go for it! Like Pop always says, 'Whatever tickles your toes.' "

Beth finally walked up. "Another Bud?"

"Yeah," he told her.

"You want another Miller, Ann Marie?" Beth asked.

"No, I'm fine. Thanks, though."

"Be right back," Beth told Billy.

"You know, she's kinda cute," Billy said as he watched Beth walk away. "Is she dating anyone?"

"Why? Are you interested in her?" Ann Marie raised one eyebrow and asked.

"No, of course not. I was thinking about my buddy, Canonball. He and his girlfriend back in Tupelo have split. I just thought he and Beth might hit it off, that's all. She kinda strikes me as Canonball's type. Tall, skinny, and religious."

Ann Marie turned around and looked across at Beth. She was standing at the bar, waiting on her orders. "Well, I'm not really sure if she's seeing anyone or not. I'll be happy to ask her, though, if you want me to."

"I don't know. Just a thought. Probably won't be seeing Canonball much more anyway."

"Why would you say something like that?"

"Why do you think? I've been expelled, remember? It's over. I'm outta here."

"So, this is it? You're just going to leave Oxford?" she demanded to know.

"What choice do I have, Ann Marie? I've just been *fired* from college. How did I know this jerk was the chancellor's damn nephew? Just my friggin' luck." Billy pulled his pack of Winstons from his shirt pocket and lit one with a match.

"Would it really have made any difference if the guy hadn't been related to Chancellor Wright, Billy?"

"Hell, no. I'd still have kicked his butt for what he was trying to do to you."

"And you'd still have gotten in trouble, just the same. Don't you see this?"

"No, I don't. Besides, what does it matter now?"

Ann Marie didn't say anything. She let go of Billy's hand and took the last sip of her bottle of warm beer. She said she looked around the new pizza place for a while, checking out the crowd inside and thinking to herself, praying for the guidance to be able to help the man she loved more than anyone else in the world. Then Ann Marie looked back at Billy. "Didn't Dean Montgomery say you could reapply again, next summer?"

"Yeah, right. Get real, Ann Marie. I'm totally screwed. They'll never let me back in here. You know this. I'll probably have to go to Mississippi State now. *Damn.*"

"No, I don't know this, Billy, and neither do you."

"Trust me, I know. This isn't the first time."

"What do you mean?" she asked him, warily.

"I mean, this isn't the first time something like this has happened to me. It's happened before." Billy took a drag from his cigarette. He looked around the restaurant and waved at Beth to hurry up and bring him his fourth beer. "I…I've been expelled before. For fighting."

Ann Marie peered into Billy's light blue eyes. She said she was almost afraid to ask him to explain, but she did.

"I hurt this black guy last year at Tupelo High

School. Pretty bad. I didn't really mean to. I mean, I meant to beat him up, teach him a lesson, you know, because…because of something he did. But I didn't mean to hurt him so bad. I promise I didn't. I don't know, I guess I just don't know when to stop. I guess, well, maybe I don't know how to, you know, control my temper."

"Have you ever talked to anyone about this, Billy?"

"My temper? Sure, for what it was worth. A counselor in junior high school, one in high school—oh, and Reverend Gillespie, at our church. My folks even sent me to this so-called 'child psychologist' up in Memphis, seven or eight times. He was a damn fruitcake, though. All any of them ever did was to just make me feel more guilty."

"Guilty? Guilty about what?" Ann Marie said she asked Billy.

Beth walked up with Billy's fourth and final Bud. Billy checked his watch. "Bring me the tab, will ya?"

Ann Marie said she was surprised Billy would want to leave before closing time. This wasn't normally like him. "Billy, this black guy over in Tupelo you got in a fight with last year, what was it all about?"

Billy took a swig from his cold can of beer, a long drag from what he thought would be his last cigarette in there, then put it down in the ashtray next to him. "Well, it really wasn't about something he *did*. It was about something he *said*."

"What was it he said?"

"It was something he said about Pop. Something totally wrong. As wrong as wrong gets."

"Pop? You mean your father?"

"Yeah. I've called him this ever since I was a kid.

He used to call his ol' man this, too. Funny, huh?" Billy took another chug. "Anyway, Pop really is a great guy. He just has this, this problem, you know. And it was something this dude, Lavonne, said about him. He spread it all over school. He told everybody—my friends, teachers, coaches, anyone who would listen to the damn pothead."

"Billy, please listen to me for a second." Ann Marie put her hand on Billy's arm. "I don't really know much about your parents or your past, and I frankly don't care. All I know is this: I don't believe in judging people because of their parents, their past, their habits, or anything else. All that truly matters is what's inside a person's heart.

"And despite all the hurt and anger I know you struggle with, I can see the goodness inside yours. I love you, Billy, and I want to help you. It's all that matters to me."

"But my parents are a part of me too, Ann Marie, both of them."

"So what? You're still you."

Ann Marie said Billy began to get agitated. "Ann Marie, you're not listening to me. I almost killed that prick last night! I almost killed Lavonne last year in Tupelo! Don't you see the pattern here?"

"Those were both accidents, Billy. You just told me you didn't mean to—"

"No, I was *lying* to you...they weren't just accidents. I *did* mean to. I *wanted* to kill them. Don't you get it? I'm a liar, Ann Marie, just like my mother's always said!"

"That's not true, Billy. You're not a liar. I don't believe this. And as far as last night goes, you...you were just protecting me. You were just angry, that's all."

"But that's my point, Ann Marie. This is what I'm trying to tell you! I'm *always* angry. I'm angry during the day, at night—hell, I'm even angry in my dreams." Billy swigged a long swallow of beer. Then he set the Bud can back down on the table. He bent over and stared at it, obviously in deep thought.

"What happened last year in high school, Billy? What did this Lavonne guy say about your father?"

Ann Marie said Billy just kept staring at his beer. He finally straightened up in his chair and spoke without ever looking at Ann Marie, expressionless, mechanical, like he was being interrogated by a cop.

"My, uh, father drinks. He drinks a lot. I guess...I guess Pop's probably an alcoholic. Mother and my Grandmother Justice both claim he is. I don't know; they're probably right. Anyway, he, uh, got drunk one night after work. He had a car wreck. It was all his fault. He hit this kid. This little black kid riding on his bike. The kid was hurt. Pretty bad. He almost died. My father got in a lot of trouble. He went to jail. He got fired from the insurance company he used to work for. We got sued. Pop had to find another job. This is why they moved down to Natchez. To try to escape, forget—start all over again."

"Billy, a lot of people drink, and a lot of people get drunk," Ann Marie told him. "That's nothing for you to feel guilty about. So what, your father has a drinking problem? It's not *your* fault. People do what they want to do, what they choose to do. My dad and my stepmother both drink, and I'm sure they've probably both been drunk, several times."

"This black guy, Lavonne," Billy stated as he continued to look away, like he wasn't even listening, "he spread it all over school that Pop *intentionally* tried to run this little boy over, that my pop was a racist who hated blacks, and it really *wasn't* an accident. And, hell, Lavonne was one of my best friends! I still can't believe he would have done something like this. It was all just a damn lie! Pop doesn't *hate* anybody. Hell, he doesn't even hate me for, for—"

"For what, Billy?"

"For what I did."

"*For what you did…?*" Ann Marie said she sat there for a second, trying to comprehend what Billy had just said and why. She reached across the table and gently touched Billy's right cheek. She tried to read his eyes. "Why would your father possibly hate you? All you did was take up for him, just like you took up for me."

"No. That's not what I'm talking about."

"Then what? Why would your father hate you, Billy?"

Billy looked away. "I can't talk about this, Ann Marie. Ever. I wouldn't even tell my shrink about what I did. I couldn't. It just hurts too much."

Billy took a hit from his smoke and chugged the rest of his Bud. "I'm leaving for Natchez tomorrow, Ann Marie. I guess I'll have to borrow someone's truck. My things won't all fit in my small Ford," Billy told her. "I'll call my friend Andy. Yeah, I bet he'll let me borrow his truck; he owes me a favor. Sorry, but there's nothing more for me here at Ole Miss, Ann Marie." Billy looked down at his Budweiser, dejectedly. He took a swallow. "I'm outta here—"

"Look at me, Billy Hall. Look at me, damn it!"

"What?" Billy looked up from his beer and faced Ann Marie.

"I can't believe you just said this!"

"That I'm leaving tomorrow?"

"No, that there's nothing here for you. You can't be serious! What about me? Don't I mean *anything* to you?"

"You know you do, Ann Marie. I love you."

"Then prove it!"

"How more can I possibly prove it to you than by what I did last night?"

"By staying here. If you really love me, Billy, then why would you leave me?"

"Because I don't have any other choice."

"No, you do! You *do* have a choice. You can stay up here."

"What the hell am I gonna do up here now? They kicked me out of school. Or have you already forgotten?"

"Billy, Billy, listen to me. Please... You can get a job and work up here. Save some money, like Beth. She's not taking any classes this summer."

"You don't understand."

"Then help me, Billy," she begged him. "Help me to understand. Please!"

"My mother...she said I have to move down to Natchez with them."

"Your *mother*? What does your mother have to do with this?"

"I just told you, Ann Marie. My mother's ordered me to pack my bags and come to Natchez tomorrow. She told me so on the phone this afternoon. I can't disobey her. I can't."

"You're kidding me, right? *That's* why you're leaving…because your mother *ordered* you to? My God, Billy, you're a grown man! You don't have to do what your mother tells—"

"I wish it were so simple." Billy's Winston had gone out in the ashtray, so he lit another one. He exhaled two huge smoke rings, which Ann Marie claimed floated to the ceiling. "You don't know her, Ann Marie. You don't know what she does, how she makes you feel."

Ann Marie stared at Billy in amazement. "How *does* she make you feel, Billy?"

Billy thought for a few seconds. "How does she make me feel? How does she make me feel?" He smirked. "Hell, that's what my damn shrink up in Memphis used to ask me, too. 'How does your mom make you feel, son, when she says all those mean things? When she screams at you, spanks you, and locks you in your room all day?' Man, talk about an idiot! What the hell did he expect me to say?" Billy looked into Ann Marie's desperate eyes. "Mother makes me feel like killing myself. That's how she makes me feel. Just like I used to tell my shrink: 'Like I never should have been born.' Does this answer your question?"

Ann Marie said she was speechless. She looked away and bit her lip to keep from saying something she knew she would later regret. She prayed silently for the strength to not hate our mother for whatever this whole, horrible mess was all about, which she said she wasn't sure if she even wanted to know. Then tears started to glisten in Ann Marie's eyes for this man-child, my older brother, whom she so dearly adored and instinctively wanted to rescue.

Finally, Ann Marie looked back at Billy. "So this is it, then. This is 'Goodbye.' Just like that. After nine months of being together, almost every day and night, and you're just walking out of my life—like none of it ever happened. Like none of it even *matters*! Is this what you're saying to me, Billy? Is it, damn it?"

Billy put his Winston down in the ashtray. He took Ann Marie's right hand between his. Her tiny hand was shaking. "You don't understand, Ann Marie. I have to do what Mother tells me to. We all do. That's just the way it is."

Ann Marie withdrew her hand. "You're right—I *don't* understand! I don't understand at all! Mainly, though, Billy, I don't understand you!"

Ann Marie said she leaned over and put her hand on his cheek again. She held it there as she tried once more. "But I do understand this: I love you, Billy Hall. I don't want to lose you. I want to be with you. I don't care about your past. I only care about our future…together."

Billy removed her hand from his cheek. He held it again and kissed it twice. Ann Marie said she began to cry. "If you love me, Ann Marie, then let me go. Let me do what I have to do. Please, please… I have to go. I'm sorry."

Ann Marie shook her head as tears slid down both her cheeks. "No, no, Billy. I can't. I just can't. I'm afraid. I'm afraid I'll never see you again—that I'll lose you forever."

"That's ridiculous, Ann Marie," she said Billy told her. "I'll come back. I promise you I will. We'll still be together…always. Plus, I'll have to return the truck to Andy—"

"No. I'm going with you." Ann Marie withdrew her right hand and wiped her eyes with a napkin. "I'll drop out this summer too. I'll go to Natchez and find a job, get an apartment down there until you—"

"No. No!" Billy said, abruptly. "You can't. I mean, you can't just up and quit school. What would your father think?"

"I don't care what my father thinks. I'm a grown woman. And I don't care about school. I care about you, Billy. Don't you get it?"

"No, Ann Marie, no! Listen to me. This is not a good idea. Not now. You have to trust me on this."

"Why not? I want to meet your parents, Billy. I want to get to know them. Your little brother Charlie, too. And I want them all to know just how much I love—"

"Where is Beth with the tab?" Billy asked, changing the subject. Billy reached into a pocket of the same cut-off jeans he had been wearing the night before. They had dried blood stains on them from the fight. He pulled out a ten and a five, enough for both the bill and the tip, and put them under his empty beer can. "I don't want to talk about this anymore. Let's go. It's getting late, and I have to start packing."

Billy took a last drag from his Winston, then he snuffed it out. He got up and helped Ann Marie from her chair. She told us everyone in Cangemi's could probably tell she had been crying, so she lowered her head as she and Billy walked toward the entrance, hand in hand.

Ann Marie said Billy noticed Beth watching them

as they made their way through the crowd. He yelled over the revelry at Beth and motioned with his right hand to tell her he had left some cash for her on the table. Beth smiled and nodded her thanks back to Billy, but her eyes were focused on Ann Marie. She continued to stare at her friend from her Spanish class while Billy opened the door and let two couples inside. Then they left Cangemi's Pizza Place.

As they were walking toward her car, Billy looked at Ann Marie and asked, pensively, "Do you believe God punishes us for our sins?"

Ann Marie said she stopped dead in her tracks as Billy continued to walk. "No," she told him, flatly. "I don't." Billy finally stopped and turned around to face her. "I *don't* believe this. I never have and never will. Why would you even ask me such a question, Billy?"

"It's kinda been on my mind, lately." Billy was searching her eyes. "Just wondering, that's all. Forget I even asked. I'm sorry," Billy said for the second time, Monday night.

"Sorry for what, Billy?" She told us she asked him, but Billy never answered her.

Later, as we sat around the parlor and listened intently to Ann Marie's story, Tillie remarked, "You know, an apology can never change the past, but it can alter the future."

Hank and Tillman both nodded in agreement. So did everyone else.

Chapter Eight

I cried and cursed, and I beat my pillow to death until I finally fell asleep about ten o'clock, Monday night. When I snored suddenly and woke myself up from my escape from Mother's hell, I had been snoozing face down on my pillow. The light in my room was still on. I hadn't undressed and turned on my overhead fan, so my pullover shirt was drenched in sweat. I rolled over on my back and stared up at the ceiling fan light. I started to get out of bed to turn it off and undress so I could drift off to Heaven again. When I glanced over at my alarm clock, I noticed it was almost twelve. *Tillman*! I suddenly remembered. *He told me to meet him at twelve*!

I got up out of my bed and slowly, quietly, crept the ten feet down the hall to the smelly bathroom. As I tiptoed past my parents' bedroom, I thanked God their door was closed and prayed they were sound asleep. I walked into the bathroom and gently closed the door behind me. I turned on the light and quietly lifted the commode seat, then carefully peed on the side of the toilet, to not rustle the still murky water.

I certainly knew better than to flush it and wake my parents. I was aware of Mother's big ears, but I was unaware Dad was still passed out on the sofa in the den, dead to the world. When I checked myself in the mirror, I really didn't have too bad a bed head, since I had been sleeping on my stomach. I even considered brushing my teeth, but then I quickly decided my breath probably smelled great compared to Tillman's and Hank's breaths, and, besides, spirits couldn't smell, much less actually care.

I tiptoed back up the hall to my bedroom, closed the door, and walked over to my dresser. First, I changed shirts, then I picked up the Hershey bar Grandmother Justice had packed, unwrapped it, took a big bite, and savored the taste of saliva and chocolate in my mouth. And even if my breath did stink, what could possibly smell better to anyone, human or spirit, than the sweet smell of chocolate? I rewrapped the Hershey bar so I could eat some more of it later, and then I stuck it in the pocket of my shirt so it wouldn't melt. I turned out the light, walked over to my window, opened it, and carefully crawled outside.

I had forgotten how tall Tillman was, and I fell to the ground on my back. No damage was done, even to the Hershey bar, and this was what I was most concerned about. I slowly closed the window, leaving a small crack for my return, later that morning. As best I could in the darkness, I brushed the dirt off my back and butt, and then I walked across our front yard until I stood at the edge of the street.

There was a full moon out again, and it was more than bright enough to read my watch. It was three minutes after twelve, the start of my third day in Natchez and the second greatest adventure of my life. Across the street, I could see Hank sitting on the top step of the Dawes' mansion, smoking a cigarette. He was wearing the same priest clothes I had seen him in earlier, but his white collar was undone, and he wasn't wearing his priest jacket.

At first, I didn't think Hank had noticed me, since he only had one eye, but then he waved his hand in the air for me to come join him. For a moment, I considered turning around, running back to my house, and crawling through my window to the relative safety of my own room, but I didn't want Hank to think I was afraid. Plus, I knew he would have told Tillman, and I didn't want to whip Tillman's butt when he started ribbing me again about being chicken, since we were sort of becoming friends now.

Hank told me later my "bold and mature decision to cross over" that night was my "great adventure," my "hero's journey," like Joseph Campbell used to write about, he told me. But I had never heard of this Campbell guy then, so I attributed Hank's rambling to his fried brain cells, caused by fifty years of drinking cheap vodka, like Tillman had said.

I finally gathered the conviction to be a man again. I looked both ways, walked across the street, and stood at the edge of the Dawes' front yard. I stood there staring at a rotund, bald-headed, one-eyed, inebriated ex-priest and fearing I had probably lost my young mind.

I hate to admit it, but I had always been leery of Catholics. There weren't many in Tupelo, back then, and Grandmother used to claim the Pope was probably the Antichrist and all Catholics were bound for Hell. But this seemed wrong and judgmental to me, so I wasn't going to tell Hank what she said. I would understand, later, how wrong it is to judge others and how much this displeases God, since only He can see inside our hearts. And, like Ann Marie told Billy

Monday night, this is all that truly matters. No, there was no way I was going to tell Hank how leery I was of Catholics. Plus, I was afraid he might could turn me into a toad frog, too.

Hank finished his smoke, glared at me, and flicked his cigarette butt out onto the yard. "It's about time you finally showed up, tyro!" Hank glanced down at his watch and said, loud enough to wake the dead, "I was just about to give up on you." Hank reached behind him and pulled out another half pint bottle of vodka from his back pocket, twisted the cap off, and took a swig. "C'mon up, tyro. I'm not a spook, and I certainly mean you no harm."

I decided to stay where I was. "I'm not afraid," I told him quickly. "If this is what you're thinking, Father Ishee, then you're wrong."

"Nobody ever said you *were* afraid," Hank replied calmly.

I turned around and looked back across the street at my house, aglow in the moonlight. A police car drove up. It slowed down and stopped in the road when the officer saw me standing on the curb. An older, black cop rolled down his window and asked me, "You okay there, son?"

Hank hollered from the front porch to him. "It's okay, Malachi! His name's Charlie Hall, Tillman's new friend. He moved in with his parents across the street in Mr. Abrams' old house. Just coming over for a late-night rendezvous."

Malachi obviously knew Hank, so he waved an Okay to him. "Just don't you be out rendezvousin' too late, you hear?" he told me.

"No, sir, I won't," I told Malachi the cop as he

rolled up his window and proceeded down Melrose Avenue.

"There's no point considering going back home now. I'm afraid it's too late for this. You've already crossed the River Jordan, so to speak," Hank said. He took a quick sip from the vodka bottle and lit another cigarette.

I swallowed a huge lump in my throat. "I was looking for Tillman, Father Ishee. Do you know if he's up yet?"

"Up? The damn boy's always up. Don't you mean, tyro, is he awake yet?"

"Yes, sir. Sorry. That's what I meant. Is he?"

"He never went to sleep. He's working tonight."

"Working? Working where?"

"Inside. He's on duty now. So I get to take the rest of the evening off and enjoy this lovely night. Ah, yes, tyro—a clear May night with a brilliant full moon lighting up the world. One of God's greatest gifts to us mortals, don't you think?" Hank pointed with his cigarette up to the sky. "Just look at that moon. If this isn't a miracle from God, then I don't know what is."

"I don't believe in miracles," I quickly let him know.

Hank was in the process of taking a sip from his bottle again when I said this. He stopped and put the bottle back down on the porch. He rubbed his chin and studied me for a few seconds.

"Well, now, a precocious young man who believes in spirits but doesn't believe in miracles. That certainly is a curious paradox. How do you reconcile this, tyro? I thought I'd pretty well heard it all, but I don't quite follow—"

"I wish you'd quit calling me 'tyro,' Father Ishee. My name is—"

"Yes, I know. 'Charlie,' " Hank said.

"Right. Charlie."

"I'll make you a deal. If you'll call me 'Hank,' I'll call you 'Charlie.' Deal?"

"Deal."

"By damn, Charlie and Hank it is, then!" Hank slapped his knee with his hand. "Sounds like a winner to me!"

I wasn't so sure about this, though. "So, Hank, can I please talk to Tillman? I really need to ask him something. It's kinda important."

"Yes, Charlie, I'm sure it is, and of course you can. They oughta be through in about..." Hank glanced down at his watch again. "Ten minutes. So why don't you just come up here on the porch and join me? We'll just visit a while and wait on Tillman together. Okay?"

I thought for a second or two. "Well, okay. I guess."

"Excellent!" Hank waved with his cigarette hand for me to come on up. He took three quick drags from his smoke and thumped it with his middle finger, about ten feet out in the grass.

I walked across the yard and stopped at the bottom of the steps. A warm breeze had just whisked through, and the brass wind chimes on the left end of the porch started clanging.

Hank noticed me staring at them. He cocked his slick head over toward them. "You like my new wind chimes, down there? Sound good, don't they? Just bought them last month at Woolco. Only cost me ten bucks. Not bad, huh?"

"Woolco? I thought Tillman said those chimes were—"

"Were what?"

"Aw, never mind." I walked up the four wooden steps and sat down next to Hank and his bottle. "It's really no big deal."

Hank and I sat there in silence for a minute or so, both of us staring up at the full moon and the billions of stars in the sky.

"I envy Tillman," I finally said to him.

"Go on."

"'Cause both his parents are dead. He doesn't have to watch them fight, or ever get yelled at by his mother."

"I see…" Hank got a stern expression on his face. He looked over at me. "Charlie, did Tillman tell you his parents were dead?"

I nodded.

"Let me tell you something. I wouldn't be too quick to envy Tillman, if I were you. His parents aren't dead. At least, Tillie and I don't *think* they are."

"Tillman told me his parents had been Christian missionaries to China, and they were both killed in a plane crash."

"This is just what Tillman *wants* you to believe. I don't know where he got *that* story from. He told his biology teacher in March his parents were millionaires and living in Hawaii. The damn boy would lie to Pope Paul himself—God bless his Catholic soul."

"Why would Tillman lie like this, Hank?"

"Who knows? Tillie claims Tillman's just the inevitable result of some weak sperm and a bad egg. Personally, I think his parents should have chosen *coitus interruptus* for the evening."

"Why would Tillie say this? Isn't she his great-aunt? And what's 'coitus interruptus?' "

"Certainly not. Tillie's no more his great-aunt than I am. And get your father to explain."

Hank took a swig from his bottle and fired up another Marlboro Red. "One of our clients brought him to us late one night as a gift to the spirits for what Tillie had done for her. Tillman's real mom was just a teenager, about sixteen or so, and she had the prettiest red hair I've ever seen. She had gotten pregnant and was in some sort of trouble with the police. His father was a bum and had already flown the coop before Tillman was born. The poor girl's parents had kicked her out, and she didn't know what to do with a new baby, much less how to support it. So Tillie, being the fine Christian lady she is, took him in, named him after Oliver and her, and raised him as her own."

"Has Tillie ever told Tillman the real truth? Or does he know it and just won't admit it?"

Hank took a long drag and tried to blow a smoke ring. He couldn't, so I decided to ask my dad or Billy one day if they would show him how. Hank stroked his bald head, and I could tell he was pondering how to answer my question.

"The real truth. The *real truth*… Ah, *Veritas…the Mother of Virtue*! Now that's an erudite question, if I've ever heard one. So just what do you think the real truth is, Charlie?"

I had to study on this one for a while. "Well, I guess the real truth is what you can see, what you can hear, touch, and taste with your own senses."

Hank just grunted and didn't say a word. He

looked up at the bright sky. "Have you ever seen a rainbow, Charlie?"

"Sure I have. Lots of times. Why?"

"Do you know every person sees the colors of a rainbow differently?"

"Really? Why's this, Hank?"

"'Cause we all see the rainbow from a different angle."

"No kiddin'?"

"Yep, no kidding." Hank took another sip from the bottle. "And I'll tell you something else, Charlie Hall, if you're interested, that is."

"'Course I am. Tell me, Hank."

"Good. I've always had this phobia about boring other people. Anyway…do you know why fluorescent things glow under a black light, or why bumblebees see colors people can't even imagine?"

"No… Why?"

"Because black light is ultraviolet. This means it's outside our natural range of vision. Like the bumblebees' colors. Do you understand what I'm trying to tell you here, Charlie?"

"Yes, sir, I think so. Kinda like a dog can hear things we can't because they're too high-pitched for us. Right?"

"Basically, though horses can hear even better than dogs. Anyway… So even though we might not see what someone or something else sees or may not be able to hear it or even *imagine it*, this doesn't necessarily mean the thing itself doesn't exist. Does this make any sense?"

I needed a little time to consider what Hank had just told me. I let him finish his smoke in silence, and

Hank didn't say anything else for two or three minutes. When he finished smoking, he flipped his cigarette into the front yard again and polished off the last of the vodka.

"Charlie," he finally said, "look out in the front yard. All around you."

I looked. "Okay."

"Now, tell me what you see. Look hard."

"I don't see anything, except for the dark."

"Right. But do you know what the *real* truth is, Charlie Hall?"

"No, sir. What?"

"There's a *whole* other world out there, Charlie—all around us—just waiting to be discovered! Smack dab in the midst of rejoicing saints and trembling sinners!"

I started looking around for all those saints and sinners, and then I felt stupid when it finally dawned on me what Hank was trying to get me to understand. "Are you talking about ghosts? I mean, spirits?"

"You got it."

"All around us?"

Hank nodded.

"Right this very moment?"

Hank nodded again. "Right this very moment."

"Well, then, I'm kinda glad I *can't* see 'em." I looked into his gray, right eye. "Can Tillie see them, Hank? Tillman said she can. Or was he just lying about this, too?"

"Oh, no, he didn't lie to you about that one. She can see them, all right, and communicate with them, and even help others to see them, too. This is, if they sincerely believe and, *mainly*, are willing to pay for her services." Hank burped. "Excuse me."

"How?" I asked Hank. "How does she do it?"

"She just has the gift. She always has, as far as I know. See, Tillie was born with a veil over her face, and she was the seventh daughter of a seventh daughter, so both those things make her *special*—spiritually speaking, anyway. I know it sounds far out, Charlie, but it's true."

"Damn."

"Now, didn't your mama teach you to never curse around a Catholic priest?"

"No, she's Presbyterian. She doesn't like Catholics, and she doesn't trust them. Neither does my Grandmother Justice."

"She doesn't, huh? Well, she and Tillie have something in common, then, because she doesn't, either. As a matter of fact, neither do I, anymore."

"So what's Tillman doing in there, Hank?" I looked back toward the door. "He told me to meet him back here at twelve."

Hank motioned behind him. "He's still in there helping Tillie with her eleven-thirty clients. Learning the business, if you will."

"Oh, I see."

We sat there for a few moments, both of us lost in our thoughts. Finally, I had to ask him.

"Hank, what happened to your left eye? Why is it covered by a patch?"

"I lost it in World War Two," he said with a heavy sigh. "We were fighting the Germans over in Italy. Battle of Monte Cassino, March 1944. Awful, awful battle. So many of my buddies were killed or wounded there, like me. Piece of artillery shrapnel hit me in the left eye."

"Oh. I'm sorry."

"No, don't be. Italy's where I found religion. Unfortunately, I lost it in New Orleans on Bourbon Street. At the Ritz Tits."

"My dad's from New Orleans. He's probably been there, too. Grandmother Justice says New Orleans is a wicked and evil place, though—like the town of Sodom in the Old Testament."

"Nah, probably more like Gomorrah, I'd say. But don't be too quick to judge, Charlie. Trust me, God doesn't approve of this."

"Are you really a priest, Hank?"

"Used to be, but not anymore." Hank looked away, so I figured he didn't want to discuss it, though Tillman had already told me why. Then he slapped his right knee again and exclaimed, "Well, Charlie, Tillman tells me you have a request of the spirits. What is it, particularly?"

"Yes, sir, I do. I already told Tillman what it is. Didn't he tell you? I just assumed—"

"Never assume anything, Charlie. We do not know what we do not know. So let's hear it, son—spit it out!"

I looked out across the front yard again, still looking for all those silly saints and sad sinners, floating around. Then I looked across the street at my house. The front porch light was on. "Well, what I want from those spirits is…I mean, what I'd really kinda like is—"

"What, Charlie, *what*? You must be specific, son!"

"Okay. First, I want everyone in school this fall to like me—to be the most *popular* kid in my class. Next, I wanna make straight A's in all my courses and never have to study a bit. Is this asking too much from Tillie's spirit friends?"

Hank lit another cigarette while he considered my two requests. After three puffs, Hank tapped his lips with his orange-stained index finger and said, "Hmmm. I don't rightly know. It's a lot to ask, even of strong spirits. What kind of a gift can you offer them, Charlie?"

"I really don't have any money. I've already spent most of my allowance this week, travelin' and all."

"Yes, yes, I do understand. But this does present a bit of a problem, now, doesn't it?" Hank said with a grimace.

"What do we do, then?"

Hank glanced down at the opened Hershey bar protruding from the top of my shirt pocket. He rubbed the stubby, gray hairs on his unshaven chin with his cigarette hand for a few seconds. "Tell you what we're gonna do, Charlie. No money, huh? I'll really have to think on this one. You will have to be totally quiet, perfectly still, while I meditate and commune with the spirits. We'll let them decide what your gift to them should be."

Hank laid his Marlboro down on the other side of him, closed his eye, and began to chant a song in some language I had never heard before. He folded his arms and bowed his bald head.

I watched him do this for about thirty seconds. I was afraid he might have passed out from all the vodka, so I leaned under his chin and whispered, "Hank, are you awake?"

"Silence! The spirits are about to speak!" he shouted. Immediately, Hank raised his head and opened his eye. He shot both his hands out in front of him, palms up, and proclaimed, "Out of the eater came something to eat! Out of the strong came something sweet!"

I sat there staring at him, totally confused. Suddenly, Hank reached over and grabbed the Hershey bar out of my shirt pocket. "This Hershey bar will do just fine, the spirits said. Thank you, young man, and bless you, they also said. Fortunately for you, Charlie, there's this one special spirit who just happens to love Hershey bars, especially those with almonds."

Hank quickly unwrapped the bar, crammed the whole thing in his mouth like he was starving to death, and then he tossed the wrapper over his shoulder. Then he burped again. "You know," Hank said, as he wiped his chocolate-covered mouth on the back of his left hand, "it's damn hard to beat a soft almond Hershey bar."

"If you say so, Hank."

"No, *they* say so."

"So does this mean they'll grant my requests?"

"Count on it. It's a done deal."

"How do you know?"

"Hey, I used to be a priest. We know stuff like this."

"But how can I be sure it'll actually happen?" I asked him.

Hank's whole countenance changed. He put his right hand on my shoulder and looked inside my soul. "You have to have faith, Charlie. You just have to believe. It's only what you *believe* will happen that ever happens."

The front door opened and out walked a man and a

woman, holding hands. I turned around to look. Tillie was following them, but she stopped inside the doorway. The man turned and spoke to her. "Thank you so much, Madam Dawes," he said, "for all your kind help."

The woman reached for Tillie's hand. She grasped it in both of hers. "Yes, how can we ever thank you enough? We're so grateful we were led to call you."

"I'm humbled to have helped," Tillie told her.

"It's so comforting to know our precious Bonnie is now at peace, isn't it, Jim?" the woman said.

"Yes, it certainly is," her husband Jim added. "Thank you, again, for contacting Bonnie for Patricia and me. We'll always be grateful."

"Believe me, Mr. Felton, it was my sincere pleasure."

Jim and Patricia Felton then each gave Tillie a goodbye hug. They both had tears in their eyes as they began to leave.

Hank leaned over and whispered, "Fine folks, those two. Yes, sir, real fine. Just lost their youngest daughter. Sad, very sad."

"What happened to her?" I whispered back.

"Hell if I know. Ask Tillman when he comes outside. But be prepared. Tillman gets very emotional about all this stuff. The boy has a tender heart, gotta hand him that. Damn shame he's so duplicitous, though. Probably the bad-egg thing I mentioned earlier."

The Feltons walked down the steps like Hank and I weren't even there. I watched them as they got into their white truck parked in the driveway, backed out onto the street, and drove away into the night. I glanced at my watch again. It was past twelve-thirty and still no Tillman. Tillie walked onto the porch and sat down next to me. She was dressed in the same black lace dress, the same black high-heel shoes, and she had the same purple wrap, or whatever it was, on the top of her head. Tillie patted me on my knee and left her hand there. I could feel the warmth of her strong hand.

"Beautiful sky out tonight, wouldn't you agree, Hank?"

"Yes, Tillie, I definitely would."

"And I assume you'd also agree there's no more of your vodka left."

"'Fraid not, my dear; 'fraid not." Hank burped a third time. "Sorry."

"Figures," Tillie quipped, staring up at the huge moon. She looked at me and smiled. "I think I sense here a nice young man who has a lot on his mind tonight."

I looked at Tillie. Her firm, warm hand was still on my knee. "How…how can you tell?" I struggled to ask her.

"I can feel it. Plus, oh, I don't know, just an older woman's intuition, I guess. Want to talk to me about it, Charlie Hall?"

I had never been the spontaneously crying type, but when I realized Tillie could see straight into my heart, my very soul, I broke down and started wailing. I couldn't stop. It was as if her touch, her presence—I don't recall what it was, but something in her unleashed a flood of tears from within me I didn't even know was there.

Neither she nor Hank said a word. They just let me get it all out. When I finally stopped crying, Tillie squeezed my knee and said, "It's okay, Charlie; it really is. You just needed to let go. Now you can tell me all about it."

I wiped both my eyes. Tillie reached inside a pocket of her dress and pulled out a white linen handkerchief. She told me to blow my nose in it. When I finished, I handed it back. "My mother hates me," I told her. "I just know she does." I began to cry again.

Tillie reached over and put her arm around my shoulder. She held me so closely I could smell the tang of an incense candle on the black knit shawl around her neck. I could hear her heartbeat. She kissed me softly on top of my head. "Oh, no, Charlie, no. Your mother doesn't hate you. She just doesn't know how to *love* you, that's all.

"Let me tell you something," Tillie continued. "Most folks do the best they can with what they have. Sometimes, they just don't know any better. Usually, it's not even their fault."

Tillie continued to hug me. She began to rock me while I continued to cry. Hank lit another smoke. He put his hand on my other knee and said, "It's all right, Charlie. It's all right to cry."

"You know something," Tillie finally said. "It's probably not the easiest thing in the world to move three hundred miles to a whole new town and not know a single soul. Wouldn't you agree, Hank?" Tillie asked him.

"Two hundred ninety miles. But, most definitely, my dear, most definitely," Hank said.

"And living next door to a houseful of— What was it Tillman said Charlie called us?"

" 'Crazies,' " Hank reminded her with a loud

harrumph.

"Yes, yes, that was it—*crazies*."

I was embarrassed Tillman had told them this, but Tillie tickled one of my ribs, and this stopped my sniveling. She handed me her handkerchief, again. "Here," Tillie said, "blow hard this time and dry those pretty blue eyes of yours. Gentlemen cry, but they always dry their eyes," Tillie informed me.

"That's my favorite line from the film *The Reivers*," Hank stated. "Based on Faulkner's last novel. If I recall, it won a Pulitzer Prize in 1963, and—"

"Enough, Hank. Enough. You're spoiling a special moment."

"Sorry, my dear. No disrespect meant."

I did what Tillie told me and gave her the handkerchief back.

"Now, Charlie, I'll tell you some *good* news. I have a strong hunch a certain young man, who just happens to be sitting next to me, is going to be extremely popular in school next year." Tillie tickled me again. "And make all A's with…well, maybe just a little studying."

"Really, Tillie, really?" I couldn't believe my ears.

"Really." She smiled at me. "Just believe it and do it."

I heard footsteps approaching from behind us.

"Come join us, Tillman," Tillie said, without looking behind her.

Tillman walked across the porch and plopped himself down next to Tillie. He was wearing a long-sleeved black shirt, a pair of black pants, and black shoes. "Sorry I'm so late, Hall," Tillman said as he rested his chin on his hands, his elbows propped on his knees. "I wanted to wait until the Feltons left. I just couldn't stand watching them both cry so hard."

Tillie looked at Tillman and whisked his red hair back so she could see his green eyes. They were bloodshot from crying. "They weren't sad, Tillman. Those were tears of joy the Feltons were crying. They're at peace now, too."

"But how can they be? Their daughter just drowned last week."

"I understand, Tillman," she said, "but *you* have to understand that sometimes, after a person dies, they're closer to us than they ever were before."

"I believe you, Aunt Tillie. I swear I do. I still feel sorry for them, though."

Hank yawned and scratched his big belly. He stood up and said, "Don't worry, Tillman. You'll eventually get used to it."

"Actually, Hank," Tillie told him, "I pray he never does."

Chapter Nine

Ann Marie revealed to us she had wanted desperately to stay with Billy Monday night, but Billy finally convinced her to drop him off at his dorm and go back to her apartment in town. He had a lot of packing *and* thinking to do, she said Billy told her.

It was about five in the morning when the phone rang on the nightstand next to Ann Marie's bed. Ann Marie was a light sleeper. After one ring, she was wide awake. She sat up and quickly turned on her lamp. On the second ring, she picked up the phone and said hello into it. Even before she heard his voice, Ann Marie said, she knew it was Billy calling.

"Hey. I'm sorry I woke you," Billy said into the phone. "I know it's early, but I just had to call."

She said Billy sounded different to her, calm, and at peace. "No, it's okay." Ann Marie looked around for her glasses and her wristwatch. "What time is it now, Billy?"

"A little after five."

"It's taken you this long to finish packing?"

"No. I woke up about an hour ago. I've been lying here in bed. Thinking."

"Thinking about what?" Ann Marie put on her glasses and asked.

"I need to talk, Ann Marie. It's important."

"Well, sure, Billy. Of course you can. You can

always talk to me about anything. You know this. I don't care what time it is." She brushed her long brown bangs from her eyes. "Do you want me to get dressed and come over there, Billy? I really don't mind."

"No. Thanks, though. Just stay there and listen to me. I don't want you out driving across town this early. It's still dark."

"Well, okay then. I'm listening, Billy. What's wrong?"

"Actually, there's *nothing* wrong. Everything is okay, now. But I do need to let you know something."

"What?"

"I had that nightmare again tonight, after I finished packing and went to sleep. It's what woke me up."

"Nightmare?"

"Yeah, the same one I had last night."

"I heard you saying something in your sleep last night about 'praying.' Is this what you're talking about?"

Billy didn't say anything.

Ann Marie didn't say anything.

"It's about something that happened when I was nine…something…something pretty damn bad."

"Is this the thing you didn't want to tell me about at Cangemi's, earlier this evening?"

Billy remained silent.

"Billy?"

"Uh, yeah. Yeah, it is."

"So why do you want to talk about it now, Billy? I thought you said you could never discuss it."

"Because I never *understood* it before. Now I do. It's what I've been lying here for the past hour thinking about. I understand now—it wasn't my fault, Ann

Marie. It never *was* my fault. No matter what she said."

"Who is 'she,' Billy, and what wasn't your fault?"

"My sister's death."

Ann Marie told us she went blank when she heard Billy say this. "Your sister? I never knew you had a sister, Billy. Why haven't you told me about her before?"

"Because I didn't want to."

"It hurts to talk about her death, is this why?"

"It hurts to even think about it."

"Who said your sister's death was your fault, Billy? Who would tell you such a terrible thing?" Ann Marie sat up on the edge of her bed, waiting for Billy to answer. He didn't. The only thing Ann Marie said she heard was the familiar sound of Billy striking a match to light a Winston. Then she heard him exhale a long, weary smoke sigh. "Billy, Billy?"

"Yeah. I'm still here."

"Uh, what was your sister's name?" She didn't want to ask him the same question again.

"Rebecca."

"*Rebecca*. That was my grandmother's name. How old was Rebecca when she died?"

"Eight."

"*Eight*. What happened to Rebecca, Billy? Do you feel like telling me?"

Billy told Ann Marie those questions were starting to sound too familiar. "I need to go get a beer from my fridge," he added. "I'm thirsty."

Ann Marie said she worried about Billy sneaking beer up to his room. She told us she was always afraid he might get caught and kicked out of school for such a flagrant policy violation. She also said she felt stupid when she realized this was no longer a valid concern.

Ann Marie remembered where she had left her wristwatch. She opened the drawer of her nightstand and put it on. It was five-fifteen. It seemed to her like Billy was taking forever to walk across his room to get a beer out of the small refrigerator, near the window. It belonged to Rob Sorrels, Billy's new roommate from Columbus. Canon had moved into a new apartment complex, she informed us. Ann Marie added she was glad Rob wasn't attending the summer semester there so she could stay with Billy, sometimes. Mother never even winced when Ann Marie said this.

Ann Marie finally heard Billy walking back to the telephone. She heard the familiar sound of the springs on his bed frame squeaking when Billy sat down on it. She heard him pop the top on the can. Billy took a long swallow of his Bud. Then he picked up the phone again.

"Go ahead, Billy. I'm listening," Ann Marie said to him when she could hear him breathing through her earpiece.

Billy took another drag from his cigarette and exhaled. "Like I said at Cangemi's last night, I never told the shrink up in Memphis about what happened. I was eleven when I first started going to him, since I'd been having this dream, this *nightmare*, for over a year then, off and on. Probably once or twice a week. It started several months after Sis died—that's the nickname Charlie and I used to call her…'Sis.'

"My shrink, Dr. Hal Engle was his name, tried every time I saw him to get me to tell him about my dream, but I just couldn't. I was still too ashamed, felt too guilty. I knew he already knew what happened to Sis. Mother had met with him first, and he told me she told him *how* Sis had died, just not *why*. I knew she never would."

"How did Rebecca die, Billy?" Ann Marie told us she asked him, again.

"It was Christmastime, 1969. It had snowed a few days before Christmas Day, the only time I'd ever seen this. I remember it was cold, too. *Really* cold. Christmas Eve morning, Sis and Charlie and I went outside early to play. We stayed out all day long, playing in the snow with some other kids on Clifton Street, and with these two guys who lived across the creek behind our house. You know, having snowball fights, making snow angels…just messin' around."

"How did your sister die, Billy?"

Billy took another drag and another swallow of beer. He coughed and cleared his throat. "She, uh, well, she started feeling bad, Christmas Eve night. Neither of my parents thought too much about it, at first. My mother could tell Sis was running a fever. She had the chills and a runny nose, but Gramma Justice was at our house spending the night with us that Wednesday, and she and Mother just assumed Sis had caught a cold from playing outside all day in the snow. It really didn't seem like any big deal. My pop and I were actually more concerned about Sis not feeling well enough to enjoy Santa Claus on Thursday morning."

"Billy, how did Sis die?" Ann Marie said she asked him, a fourth time.

"Mother called old Doc Bush on Friday 'cause Sis was running a high fever by then. The cold compresses on her head and the aspirins weren't helping much. Doc Bush told Mother it might be the flu but not to worry and just keep on doing what she was doing. He said the

142

flu 'had to run its course.' Two days later, Sis was even sicker, and she was coughing really bad. She couldn't seem to stop. Pop told Mother she needed to take her to see Doc Bush and get him to give her a shot of penicillin or something.

"Mother took her in to him, first thing Monday morning. Doc Bush didn't give her any medicine, though. Mother told Pop Doc Bush said the flu was a virus, so penicillin wouldn't help her. But Sis kept getting sicker and sicker. And four days later, she quit breathing." Ann Marie told us she clearly heard Billy snap his fingers together and say, "Just like that."

"We all found out later, though, after my parents had talked to some specialist in town, Sis had probably died from *pneumonia*, not the flu. When Pop heard this, he went berserk. He drove over to Doc Bush's office to beat him up, but this other doctor had already called Doc Bush and warned him. Sheriff Huff was there when Pop got to the clinic, and he and some young deputy stopped Pop from going inside. It's a good thing they did, 'cause Pop would have killed Doc Bush. My pop always blamed him for Sis's death. He probably still does. God, too.

"Pop wanted to hire this lawyer up in Memphis to sue Doc Bush for malpractice, but my mother wouldn't let him. She said Sis's death wasn't Doc Bush's fault— it was simply God's will. But I knew she was lying about that."

Ann Marie said she sat on her bed trying to figure out what Billy had meant by this. She finally said, "Billy, I'm truly heartbroken to hear this about your sister, Rebecca. I wish I had known this before. It might have helped me. I mean…maybe I would have understood—"

"No, it's okay, Ann Marie. I know what you mean. It probably would have helped me to understand me, too. I mean, if I'd realized before why I've always had this same nightmare."

"Billy, I don't understand what you mean by you 'knew' your mother was lying— What was she lying about?"

"Me."

"*You*? Billy, what did you have to do with your sister's—"

"In my dream, my nightmare, it's always the same."

"You mean, it's the same nightmare every time?"

"Right. It's always about what happened. The morning Sis died. That's what I always dream about. What I did. I mean…what I *didn't* do."

Ann Marie said she felt a sick, gnawing in her gut—a sudden, overwhelming panic like she felt the morning when her daddy came home from Reid Hospital in Meridian. As soon as he walked inside the house, before he even said a word to her or her younger sister, Mary Helen, Ann Marie could tell by the horror on his face that their precious mom had just died from cancer.

To know Billy better was something Ann Marie had once truly desired, but that early morning she feared the truth. Then, she told us, she decided to be totally honest with him. "Billy, I…I'm really trying to be strong for you, but I'm afraid I might not—"

"No, Ann Marie, no. Don't be afraid. Don't you see what I'm trying to tell you? I know now what this dream means. I understand it now, and I'll never have to dream it again."

Ann Marie said she almost didn't ask. "Uh, what…what happened the morning Sis died, Billy…what you keep dreaming about?"

"I think Mother knew Sis was dying. I don't know how I *knew* she knew. I could just sense it. She could have taken her to another doctor. Both Pop and Gramma Justice tried to tell her to, but she just wouldn't listen. Charlie was only about four, then, so Mother didn't say this to him, but she kept telling me over and over we only had to pray, we only had to pray, and Sis would get well. I never doubted it; I believed. I never even *questioned* it.

"So I started praying and praying, every night. 'God, please make my sister get well. Please don't let Sis die.' This was my prayer. I had been praying this every night for four nights, on my knees next to my bed, even on that Friday morning, January second, 1970, when Sis died. And every night I'd fall asleep on the floor from praying for so long.

"It was about ten-thirty, New Year's night, and I was about to freeze. I was kneeling next to my bed, praying the same prayer, when my bedroom door opened, and Mother walked inside. I could sense something was wrong. *Bad* wrong. I think this is when I realized Mother knew Sis was about to die. I could see it in her face. She looked defeated, helpless, like someone on an airplane might look who suddenly realized they were about to crash and die.

"But when she noticed I could tell, the horrible look on her face vanished. Instantly! I don't understand how someone could possibly change their feelings so fast, but somehow she did. I looked away quickly.

Mother really, well, she really sorta spooked me, you know.

"She walked across the room to me and just stood there while I started praying again. 'God, please make my sister get well. Please don't let Sis die. God, please make my sister get well. Please don't let Sis die...'

"Mother reached down and put her hand on my left shoulder. She squeezed so hard it was bruised the next day, but there was no way I was gonna let her know she was hurting me. I just kept on saying the same prayer. She stopped me in mid-sentence and said, 'You must keep praying all night, Billy. You must keep praying, or Rebecca will die.'

"I started to cry. I started begging God—pleading with Him, 'Please, God, please, don't let Sis die! Please, please don't let her die!' I kept crying this prayer to God, over and over and over. Finally, Mother left and locked the door behind her. I knew better than to even consider leaving my bedroom, though.

"I knelt there by my bed, praying hard and crying. I cried so much that night I'm surprised I didn't wake up Charlie in his bedroom down the hall. I must have finally fallen asleep on the floor, again, because the next thing I remember is hearing a key unlocking my door. I was curled up in a fetal position next to my bed, not yet fully awake. It was about four on Friday morning.

"All of a sudden, the door flies open! My mother sees me lying on the floor. She storms over to me and jerks me up by the arm—clean off the floor—like I was a damn rag doll. I'll never, *ever* forget the look on her face. Then Mother starts screaming at me, like she was crazy. 'I told you to pray all night! You lied to me; you

lied to me! Do you want your sister to die? Do you?'
She made me kneel back down and start praying again.
'Now, *pray*—like I told you to!'

"I'm sorry, Mother. I'm sorry! I did pray. I *did*
pray! I *did*…!" Billy kept on saying.

Ann Marie said she couldn't take any more. It was
all incomprehensible to her. She told us she first tried to
convince herself Billy must be making this up because
this just couldn't possibly be true. She said she thought
maybe he was drunk and just playing a cruel joke on
her. Or maybe he had taken a hallucinogenic drug, and
he was out of his… But, no, no, she finally said, she
knew Billy too well to believe any of this. She said the
only thing she could figure was this had to be a
nightmare.

And Ann Marie was right. It was a nightmare…
both hers and Billy's.

She said she only heard Billy mumbling, after this.
She was certain Billy was speaking in a normal voice as
he kept talking about this horrifying experience he had
endured when he was only nine, but the rest of what he
said was lost on her. She had heard and imagined far
more than anyone should have to digest, and she
realized then why Billy had kept all this buried inside
him.

She also realized this was the problem. It was so
deeply buried in his heart, so ingrained in his mind, and
so scarred on his soul…how could Billy ever recover?
More than this, though, she wondered how Billy Hall
had ever survived and how she could ever rescue him.

Ann Marie said the next thing she heard Billy say
after this was Sis had died, shortly after five in the
morning.

147

Billy then started explaining to Ann Marie he knew now it wasn't his fault, that it never was. He told her it wasn't *anyone's* fault—not Doc Bush's, not Mother's…not even God's. He also told her he remembered hearing in church once that God suffers, too. So Mother was wrong, he said. It *wasn't* God's will Sis had died. It simply happened.

Ann Marie told us she felt lightheaded, dizzy, like her spirit had just left her body and floated to the top of her bedroom ceiling. As Billy kept on explaining, she said she felt a sudden sense of terror, just like when she was six and almost drowned in her uncle's swimming pool in Meridian.

The only things she could say to Billy were, "Yes, yes, I do agree," and "You're right, Billy. You're so right." She also told him several times how truly sorry she was he had experienced such a traumatic thing. But Billy told Ann Marie it was all okay—now that he finally understood, now that he was finally free, and, mainly, now that he could finally forgive God, Mother, and, most of all, himself.

Then Billy told Ann Marie he had changed his mind. He had decided to stay up there with her for the summer and work while she attended classes. Just like she had suggested.

"What, Billy? What did you just say?" Ann Marie's silver cord quickened and snapped her spirit back into her body. She said it felt like a yo-yo snapping back into her hand. "Are you serious? Please tell me you're not just kidding me!"

"Yes, I'm dead serious. I'm not listening to my mother anymore. Not ever again."

Ann Marie was speechless. She swallowed the

lump in her throat. Her broken heart started beating again. "This is great, Billy, absolutely great. But what…what made you change your mind? I mean, I just want you to be *certain* about this. I want it to be your decision, not—"

"It *is* my decision. That's my whole point, Ann Marie. From now on it's *always* going to be my decision. Mother's doesn't count anymore, or anyone else's, for that matter."

Ann Marie said this was what she had feared. She was happy Billy had finally realized he wasn't to blame for our sister's death, that he had extricated himself from our mother's guilt and oppression. But she feared his emotional pendulum had swung too far, that Billy Hall would never listen again—to anything or anyone. Including her.

"So I'm driving down to Natchez today to tell her," Ann Marie then heard him say.

"Tell her? Your mother? Tell her what, Billy?"

"What I just said— I'm staying up here. I don't need Andy's truck now. I'll drive my own car—"

"You're driving all the way to Natchez just to *confront* your mother? Just call her, Billy. There's no need for you to—"

"No, Ann Marie, not just to *confront* my mother. I need to see Charlie and Pop. I haven't seen them since spring break. Plus, I want to see their new house. And I really want to meet those weird agents Charlie told me about across the street. Who knows, that old woman might just dance—"

"I think you're being ridiculous."

"I'm just kidding, Ann Marie. Charlie said she's old enough to be—"

"No, I mean driving down there. What if, well, what if—"

"Don't worry, I'm not gonna change my mind and not come back. I promise. And my mother sure as hell isn't gonna stop me. I'm just gonna spend one night with them, and then I'll drive my car back here tomorrow afternoon."

"So you're leaving this morning, then?"

"Yeah. Actually, since I'm already up, I think I'll go jump in the shower and get an early start. I'm thinking I might—"

"I'm going with you. It won't take me long. I can be ready in thirty minutes. The only class I even care about missing is my—"

"No, no, Ann Marie, no. I told you at Cangemi's, *no*! This is something I have to do alone. It's not your time, I mean—it's not your place to help me. If you went with me, I know Mother'd just think you put me up to this. I don't want her blaming you. That's not fair to you, and it's not fair to her, either. I want her to know we're *both* free, now.

"Like I was trying to tell you, I think I'll drive over to Tupelo first and spend some time with Gramma. Haven't seen her since spring break, either. She's getting up in age, you know, and with our family having moved away, she's probably lonely now. I wanna take her out to the cemetery with me to visit Sis's grave, and Papa Justice's too. Put some flowers on both of them—and see a few ol' buddies before I head down to Natchez."

Billy had always been convincing, and Ann Marie said she was too drained to argue with him. Plus, she knew it would do no good. All she said was, "I finish my Spanish class today at three-fifty. I need to go to the library for a couple hours after it's over, but I'll be back here by six. You call me at six, okay? Collect. And don't you drive too fast or drink too many—"

"Ann Marie, don't worry about me, okay? I'm happy now."

"Billy?"

"What?"

"I love you. I love you very much. I always have."

"I know, Ann Marie. And I love you, too. I always will."

Chapter Ten

I left Tillie, Tillman, and Hank about one-thirty Tuesday morning, snuck back through my bedroom window, undressed, and finally fell asleep about two-thirty. I remember dreaming about Billy, right before I woke up.

We were kids again, about seven and twelve, and I was trying to pedal my old bicycle up this long, steep street. Billy had already pedaled his bike to the top of the hill, and he was sitting there on it, watching me as I grunted and groaned, struggling to make my way up.

Billy cupped his hands to his mouth and hollered down the hill to me, "Hurry up, Charlie! It's *beautiful* up here! I can't wait for you to see it! Sis is here, too!"

I could barely breathe as I stood up on my bike to try to pedal harder, but I managed to holler back to him, "Wait for me, Billy! I'm pedaling as fast as I can!"

"Don't worry, Charlie, I'm not going anywhere! I'm not ever gonna leave you...!"

Then I woke up, about eight, and this is what Dad told me later:

Mother was in the kitchen, scrambling eggs in a skillet. Dad walked in, adjusting his tie, and went over and kissed her on the cheek. "Already fried the bacon," Mother told him, nodding to it on two paper towels on top of the counter. "Eggs'll be ready in a minute." Mother turned and nodded at the moving box on top of the counter, next to the refrigerator. "Move this box for me, please, William. I forgot to take it out to the back porch last night."

Dad went over to the box and peered inside through one of the large holes Mother had made on the top flaps. "This little bird's really flopping around in here, Claire. Why don't you let it go? It can probably fly."

"Oh, no," Mother quickly replied. "I couldn't possibly do that. It's still just a baby, and its mama would never take it back, since I've handled it now."

Dad didn't try to reason with her. He said this was a waste of time. He picked up the box and carried it out to the back porch. "And check on Charlie for me," Mother said as he left the kitchen. "It's time for him to get up."

Mother scooped the scrambled eggs from the skillet into a bowl. She poured Dad a cup of hot coffee from the percolator on the other burner and turned them both off. She took the bowl of eggs and the coffee cup and went over and put them both down at Dad's seat. Dad came back into the kitchen and got the bacon, toast, and grits while Mother set the table. Then my dad went to get me.

I was still lying in bed, thinking about my dream about Billy, when Dad walked into the hall and knocked on my door.

"Hey, in there! You awake yet?" he yelled.

"No! Go away!"

"Get up and get dressed! It's time for breakfast."

Dad walked back up the hall, through the dining room, and into the kitchen.

"Sit down, William, and fix your plate. Is Charlie

awake yet?" Mother asked him.

"He is now," my dad told her as he sat down and scooped scrambled eggs and grits onto his plate. Then he reached for two pieces of bacon and some buttered toast. "Got any jam?"

"No, sorry. I'll get some today. I have to go to the A&P again. I want to make spaghetti and meatballs tonight. I haven't made this in a while."

"Great. Love your meatballs." Dad took a quick sip of coffee and glanced at his watch. "I'm gonna have to hurry to eat all this," he told her. "So what else do you have planned for today?"

Mother took two more pieces of toast from the toaster and buttered them. "Well, I really need to call the cable TV company to see if they're coming today. This'll give Charlie something to do, since he's grounded now."

"Funny, I haven't even missed watching television."

If I had been Mother, just then, I'd probably have said something clever back to Dad, like, "Good thing. You were too drunk last night to focus!" If I had been Dad, I'd have reminded Mother *I* was the man of the house, so *I* decided who got grounded—not her!

So much for disciples and buddies...and parents, too.

But neither one of them was obviously as clever or as brash as me. Dad kept cramming eggs and grits into his mouth, and all my mother said was, "Well, Charlie has. He'll get bored sitting around all day. And he's forbidden to ever go back over to the *Dawes* place. I told him this last night after he finally got home. You were on the couch. Passed out, as usual."

Dad said his mouth was too stuffed to respond. I told him later it was like the mover's rut in our old yard and to just forget about it, since it didn't matter. He liked this.

Still, someone had to act like a man.

Dad washed down his food with a big swig of coffee. Mother was preparing me a plate.

"I don't know where Billy's gonna sleep," Dad said. "There're only two bedrooms here."

"Yes, don't remind me. He can sleep in Charlie's room tonight with him. Charlie'll probably love that."

"What about Billy? He might not—"

"Then Billy can sleep on the new couch, since it's already been *used*. I knew better than to leave his twin bed with Mother. I don't know why I did this. I'll have it shipped down here. It'll fit next to Charlie's twin bed in his room."

Dad said he had a pounding headache Tuesday morning. He also said he didn't feel like arguing with Mother, but he wanted to finish. "What I was trying to say, though, Claire, is Billy might not want to *stay* in Charlie's room. They've had separate bedrooms since—"

"I don't care what Billy wants. Billy'll do what I tell him to do. He's brought this on himself—again, I might add."

"But where's he going to store all his things? I really think Billy should stay up in Oxford for the summer. Get a job there. I think we should discuss this with him tonight."

"There's nothing to discuss. Billy can get a job here in Natchez. He belongs at home with us." And this was the end of that, Dad said.

I walked into the kitchen wearing the same pair of cut-off shorts, no shoes, and no shirt. My blond hair was matted together like a cheap rug.

"I thought I told you to get dressed," Dad said, looking up from his plate. He took another sip of his coffee and frowned at me.

"I *am* dressed, Dad." I walked across the floor to the refrigerator. The cool linoleum on the kitchen floor felt good to my bare feet.

Mother stopped me as I opened the refrigerator door. "Go sit down at the table, Charlie. I'll get you some orange juice."

I walked over to the table and sat down next to Dad. Mother brought me a plate. "Go ahead and eat," she said. "The eggs in the bowl are still warm."

Dad leaned over and whispered, "This is not exactly what I had in mind by 'dressed.' "

"Sorry," I whispered back. "Where's the darn bird?" I asked out loud. "It was making a lot of racket last night."

"I took it out to the back porch," Dad said.

"Good. It was startin' to stink, too."

Mother asked me if I wanted some milk.

"No."

"No, *ma'am*," Dad corrected me.

"No, ma'am."

"What you gonna do today, Charlie?" Dad asked me.

His geniality was starting to get on my still-sleepy nerves by then. "Be bored... Mother, will you call the cable company today?"

" 'Please'?" Dad suggested.

"Please?" I added.

"Yes, I will. So eat," Mother said again. She glanced at the clock on the wall over the stove. "William, you better hurry. It's almost eight-thirty."

Dad took a quick bite of his toast and gulped the rest of his coffee. He looked at his watch. "I gotta get going!" He got up from the table and, as usual, ruffled my hair. "See ya, Charlie. Hope ya get the cable today." Dad walked over to Mother at the stove and hugged her.

She even hugged him back. "Go sit down and eat, Claire," he told her. "The eggs'll get cold if you don't eat some now."

"I'm really not hungry this morning. I'll get a salad for lunch. I saw this cute little restaurant downtown yesterday, and I want to try it."

"Good. Who knows, you might make a friend today. What time's Billy getting here?"

"I don't really know. Probably about five, I'd guess."

Dad picked up the keys to Ed's used Buick from a wooden bowl on the counter. "How's he getting here?" Dad asked her as he started to leave the kitchen.

"I didn't ask him," said Mother. "I assume he's borrowing a truck. He certainly can't fit everything into his small Ford."

"That makes sense. I guess he'll drive it back up there so he can get his car and return."

"I guess," Mother said. "Anything special you want for dessert, William?"

"How 'bout some more Hershey bars?" I suggested to her. Mother had no sense of humor. "Just a thought," I told her.

Dad looked at me and chuckled. Fortunately, he

did have a sense of humor. A little warped, perhaps, but at least he had one. "Surprise me, Claire," Dad told her as he walked out of the kitchen, through the dining room, and into the den toward the front door. He got his navy-blue blazer off the coat rack and put it on. As he opened the door to leave, he hollered back to the kitchen, "Call me if Billy gets here early, okay, Claire?"

"I will!" Mother yelled to him. Dad closed the front door behind him and left the house.

"Mother, my orange juice?" I asked her.

"Oh, sure," she said. "Sorry, I've just got a lot on my mind, this morning."

"Yeah, me too—like TV."

She brought me a glass of juice. She picked up Dad's things from the table. "Now, when you finish, scrape your plate, and put it and your fork in the sink for me, with your father's. Your glass, too. I'll wash them all when I get back after lunch. I need to go get ready now."

"I will."

Mother walked back to the sink, opened the cabinet underneath it, and scraped the rest of Dad's breakfast into a double-bagged A&P paper sack. She put Dad's plate, fork, and cup in the sink. "I really do miss my dishwasher," she said with a sigh. "Oh, well, maybe one day…"

I got the rest of the bacon from the paper towels and ate all three pieces. I took a couple of bites of cold eggs and grits and chugged the glass of orange juice as Mother finally walked out of the kitchen and headed for the hall.

"Charlie, do you need to use the bathroom before I get in there?" She hollered from down the hall.

"No, I've already gone," I yelled back to her.

I lied. I badly needed to go, but I figured it was worth waiting if it would help get my mother out of the house quicker. I knew I had a big day ahead of me.

Mother walked into the den about thirty minutes later, and it was a good thing she did, since I was having wicked thoughts about standing on a chair and peeing in the kitchen sink.

I probably would have, too, but since we didn't have a dishwasher, my plate and glass and fork were in there, also.

Mother was immaculately dressed. She had sprayed perfume all over her body, and her hair was in a bouffant, which was stiff as her neck. I was sitting on the sofa, flipping through the pages of a new *National Geographic* magazine, hoping it might have a few pictures in there of naked women in Africa. All it had in it, though, were naked guys and gazelles.

"Now, I've already called the cable company, Charlie," she said, "but just in case they don't come again today, do you want me to rent you a good book from the library or get some magazines for you to read?"

"Maybe a few back issues of *National Geographic* from the library. I like to read the articles in those."

"Really? How interesting. So does your father. Sure, I'll be glad to. Anything else?"

"Yes, ma'am. Four or five more Hershey bars."

"No. There're chocolate cookies in the pantry. This will do. There's bologna and some mayonnaise in the refrigerator. Milk, too, and plenty of bread and chips in the pantry."

"Got it. So, Mother, what time you gettin' back

home?"

"Why? You're not planning on leaving the house, I hope. You better not. In case you've forgotten, you're grounded."

"For how long?"

"For as long as I say."

"No, ma'am, I haven't forgotten."

"Good. I'll be leaving, then. I should be back by one."

"Bye, Mother. Oh...don't forget the *National Geograph*—"

"I won't. Goodbye." She opened the front door, locked the handle knob on it, and left.

When I heard her shut the door to the station wagon and crank the ignition, I got up from the sofa and walked to the front window. I separated the venetian blinds and peered through.

After Mother checked her lipstick in the rearview mirror, she turned around in the seat and backed down the driveway. She put the control stick in drive and slowly sputtered away.

"*Yes!*" I shouted. I ran out of the den, down the hall, and shot into the bathroom. The commode seat was down from Mother's having used it. I peed so hard and splashed so much water and pee on the toilet seat that now I understand why women hate men.

After I finished relieving myself, I raised the bathroom window blinds and looked out. A large oleander bush covered most of my view, but I could still see the Dawes' home across the street. I wondered if any of them were awake yet, but then I noticed their old black Lincoln Continental wasn't parked in the driveway, so I assumed Hank or Tillie must have left.

Probably for cigarettes and vodka, I figured.

I took off my shorts and kicked my underwear off my feet. I decided I really should take a shower, since Billy was coming home that afternoon. Three days without bathing was long enough. I turned around to the bathroom mirror and took a long look at my naked young body. Like Billy, I may have been short for my age, but I was glad I had muscles and wasn't just skinny, like Tillman. *Of course, I'll be popular when school starts in September*, I told myself. *Heck, who wouldn't want to hang out with someone who looks as good as me?*

Then I started feeling guilty. I had just lied to my mother, again. Stay in this house all day? No way. Besides, like Dad said, guilt was for Catholics—not Presbyterians. Plus, I had a major request of Tillie's spirit friends, and this time it wasn't for me.

This was bound to make my three lies to Mother okay, I convinced myself. I turned on the shower, sniffed both my underarms, and stepped inside. I wondered when the blond hairs underneath them would start to grow longer, like the hairs on another place on my body.

I finished my shower and decided to try some of Dad's deodorant, like he had been suggesting for the past few weeks. *Maybe this'll help the hairs to grow? At least it'll help with the stench,* I thought. *And who knows, maybe spirits can smell.* I already knew they could taste.

After this, I brushed my teeth, brushed my hair, and got two of Mother's Q-Tips and cleaned all the wax from my ears. Then I sprayed some of Dad's Right Guard deodorant under both arms and put on some of his Old Spice cologne. I left the bathroom and walked up the hall to my bedroom, smelling pretty good, I thought.

My tan shirt was lying on the floor next to my socks, but they all stunk too bad to wear them again. So I put on some clean underwear, a clean pullover shirt, and a pair of clean white socks from my dresser. I stretched out the shirt neck to keep it from messing up my hair, pulled it over my head, and got another pair of shorts. I put on my tennis shoes and laced them both up, took another admiring stare at myself in the mirror, and then left my room.

It was a great day to be alive, thirteen, and redneck. Even in Natchez.

I went back into the kitchen before I left the house. I remembered Mother had said there were some chocolate cookies in the pantry. Since I didn't have any more Hershey bars, I prayed Hank's spirit friends liked chocolate cookies, as well as they liked chocolate candy.

Instead of leaving through the front door, I decided it might be more inconspicuous if I made my getaway from the rear. When I opened the kitchen door and walked out onto the back porch, I could smell it, and I heard it flopping around in the box my dad had taken out there and set on the floor. I really didn't blame the bird for being so upset, though, and it was probably hungry, too, because I doubted it had been fed that morning. I felt sorry for it—even though the thing stunk worse than one of Dad's painful poops.

So I changed my mind and went back into the kitchen to get the food Mother had bought for it. When I came back out onto the porch, I walked over to the box and started to drop some food inside through one of the holes; instead, I leaned over and tried to see what kind of baby bird it was.

The box was too dark for me to see inside, so I slowly opened one of the flaps. I figured the thing could probably fly, and if it got out, I knew I'd be in big trouble. So just to make sure, I looked all around the screened porch for holes the bird might escape through. I also checked the screen door for holes. Fortunately, there were none I could see.

When I opened a flap and some light shined through, I knew immediately it was a mockingbird. This wasn't one of my favorite birds, since the darn things are mean. And it was common knowledge, at least among north Mississippi rednecks, that a full-grown mockingbird would swoop down on a kid just as quickly as it would on a dog or a cat. So I was probably as leery of a mockingbird as I was of a Catholic. Except, now, for Hank.

But when the mockingbird saw me, I think it was scared. It hopped over to one corner of the box and just lit there like it was afraid to turn around and face me. "Hey, don't be scared," I told it. "I'm not gonna hurt you. I just wanna feed you. Here…" I opened the paper sack and dropped some food inside. "See…I'm just giving you some breakfast. Don't be afraid. I don't mean you any harm."

The baby mockingbird turned around, stood there in the corner of the box, and looked at me. It was like it understood what I had said to it. I picked up some food from the bottom of the box and offered it in the palm of my hand. The mockingbird hopped over and plucked the food, then swallowed it as quickly as Hank had gobbled my Hershey bar, the previous night.

The innocence and trust of this moment from my youth is something I'll never forget. The mockingbird and I stared at each other for several seconds. I somehow sensed it was big enough to fly away and fend for itself. I wanted to set it free. I *had* to set it free. I knew how it felt to be trapped, confined, and in bondage to something or someone else.

I knew I shouldn't have done it, but I just had to. I decided I didn't care anymore what my mother thought or even what she might do when she got back home and realized I had set her captive free. To my mind, the mockingbird's freedom mattered more. I picked up the box, unlocked the screen door, and walked down the two steps out into our back yard.

I set the box on the grass and opened the other three flaps, then reached down inside and picked the mockingbird up with my hand. When I opened my hand, instead of it immediately flying away, the bird cocked its small, gray head and stared at me. It was unbelievable. And for the first time in my life, I realized I had just witnessed a miracle.

I lifted my hand to Heaven, and the baby mockingbird flew away.

I knew my sin would eventually find me out, so to put off Mother's retribution as long as possible, I took the empty moving box back inside to the porch and closed all the flaps. I took the bag of food into the kitchen and put it back where I had found it, and then I got the bag of chocolate cookies and left the house through the back porch. I decided I would tell Mother when she returned I had fed her bird that morning, and it was now doing fine. This would be my fourth lie of the day; however, it was also the truth.

There would be more lies to follow, though.

I walked around the front of our house and hid for a while by one of the two crabapple trees that stood at both corners of the house. When the coast was clear, I sneaked across our front yard, checked both ways for traffic and ice cream truck hippies, and ran across the street. I didn't stop until I stood at the front door of the Dawes' antebellum home.

I turned the doorbell key twice and waited at least a minute. No response. I twisted it a third time and tried to see through the lace curtains behind the glass. Finally, Tillman opened the door. He had on a baggy pair of jeans, a wrinkled yellow shirt, and a pair of worn out flip-flops on his long feet. His toenails needed cutting even worse than his fingernails.

"What are you doing here so early, Hall?"

"It's not early. It's nine-forty-five."

"That's still early around here."

"Can I come in?"

"Yeah, I guess, but be quiet. Hank's still asleep."

I walked inside, carrying the bag of cookies, as Tillman closed the front door behind me. I looked closely at him. I thought again how proud I was I had more muscles than Tillman, and he was already fourteen-and-a-half.

"Why are you staring at me? You jealous I'm six inches taller than you?"

"Who, me? Heck, no, I'm not jealous of you about anything."

"Well, 'envious' is probably a better word, then. Who knows, Hall, you might just grow some in a year or two. Wouldn't worry about it, though. A lot of famous actors are actually just runts like you. Television makes you look taller and twenty pounds heavier, you know."

"I don't want to be an actor. They're all fake."

"Then maybe you can be a jockey. You like horses? My father used to breed racehorses. He made millions of—"

"I thought you said he was a missionary, Tillman."

"He was. Racing's where he made all his money, though, so he and my mom could work full time for God in Japan."

"Was this before or after they went to China?"

"Before. Dad hated Japanese food. It gave him gas. So that's why they went to China. But let's don't talk about my parents anymore, okay? Sometimes it makes me cry." Tillman began sniffing the air, like he had done on Sunday when he first walked into our dining room after we arrived. "What's that I smell, Hall? You wearing aftershave lotion? You're not old enough yet to shave. You have deodorant on too, don't you?"

"Yeah, it's Dad's. Right Guard. It's the first time I've ever worn deodorant. I'm hoping it might help my underarm hairs grow."

"'Bout time. I didn't want to hurt your feelings, but you were pretty rank last night. Hank noticed it, too, and he can barely smell a thing from smoking so much. I don't mean anything personal by it. I just thought you needed to know, since we're best friends now."

"Who said we're best friends?"

"Me. And consider yourself lucky. I'm very selective about whom I'm best friends with."

Tillman sniffed the air again. "What kind of aftershave lotion do you have on? It's not Old Spice, I hope?"

"No, it's Old Spice *cologne*."

"Well, it doesn't bother me, but don't ever wear the stuff around Tillie. She hates it. Claims it reminds her of Uncle Oliver. A smell will trigger a memory quicker than anything, you know. It's why I can't eat Japanese food. The smell of it makes me think of my parents, and I'll start crying. I'll let you borrow some of my English Leather cologne. The women love it. Turns them on." He winked one of his green eyes at me.

"Don't wink at me, Tillman. Guys don't do this to other guys."

Tillman eyed the bag of chocolate cookies in my hand. "Did you bring your breakfast with you?"

"The cookies? No, I had breakfast over an hour ago. My mother makes great scrambled eggs and bacon."

"We don't get up early enough for breakfast. Wish we did. I love eggs. Can't eat bacon, though. I'm half Jewish."

"Which half?"

Tillman pointed down at his crotch. "This half. I'm so Jewish I was circumcised twice! Get it?" Tillman laughed like a drunk idiot.

"No, and I don't want to *see* it, either. Look, Tillman, can we go sit down or something? I can't stay very long."

"Yeah, I guess, but remember…be quiet. Hank's pretty grouchy when he first wakes up. I'm always in a good mood when I get up in the morning, though."

"Me too." Not counting letting the mockingbird go, this was my fifth lie of the day, and it wasn't even ten o'clock yet.

"Let's go into the kitchen. I need my morning coffee," Tillman told me.

With a twelve-foot ceiling and two racks of copper pots and pans hanging over a butcher block table bigger than our dining room table, their kitchen was the largest I had ever seen, and I told Tillman so. Tillman said their "chef's cuisine" kitchen was probably larger than our kitchen and dining room combined, and I think he was right. He also advised me both Tillie and Hank were gourmet cooks, all their culinary talents were developed from years of living in New Orleans, and if he decided not to become a world famous decorator, then he would become a world famous chef, one day. Or maybe both, he added.

First, though, he was still learning how to make coffee. Tillman walked over to a large Mr. Coffee machine on the counter by the double stainless-steel sink, got the pot, and rinsed it out. "Wanna know how to make real coffee, Hall?"

"No, I hate coffee. I heard on TV it stunts your growth."

"Well, that's obviously a bunch of crap. Just look at me!" Tillman stood up straight and extended his skinny neck. "You need to know how to, anyway. Women really dig a guy who makes good coffee. You know, for the *morning after*." He winked his eye at me again. "Always start with a clean pot," Tillman advised as he rinsed the pot a third time. "But the main thing is," he said, swirling the tap water around and around, "after you make the coffee, always swish it around twelve times before you serve it."

"Why twelve times?"

"It's good luck. Plus, I heard Julia Child say this on

TV once, and she's the greatest chef in the world! She's half Jewish too, you know. All great chefs have Jewish blood in them."

"Never heard of her, but if I ever do start drinking coffee, I'll remember this."

"If you ever start dating, you *better*." Tillman got a large bag of coffee from the cabinet, put a filter in Mr. Coffee, put seven scoops of coffee in the filter, and turned the machine on. "It only takes eight minutes," he said. He opened another cabinet and got out a black New Orleans Saints coffee mug, rinsed it three times, set it down on the counter, and put two heaping spoons of sugar in it. "Oh, by the way, always put the sugar in first. It melts a lot faster this way. And be sure to use half-and-half, not just regular milk. It's what they do in the best restaurants in New Orleans. You think you can remember all this, Hall?"

"Probably not."

"Well, don't worry. Took me a while, too. Have a seat. I thought you said you wanted to sit down."

"Right, I did." I sat down on one of the stools next to the butcher-block table. "Thanks for reminding me, Tillman."

"So what's up, and why'd you bring those cookies over? Are they for me?"

"No. They're for Hank."

"He really likes chocolate."

"Yes, I know. So do the spirits. You can have some, too. There're plenty here."

"No, I can't eat chocolate. It gives me zits."

"You already have zits, Tillman. Duh. Is Tillie up yet?"

"She's up and gone. Why?"

"Where'd she go?"

"I don't know. She left before you woke me up. Why?"

"Just wondering."

"You come over here to see her or Hank?"

"Either one. I have another request of the spirits."

"Already?"

"It's for somebody else this time. My dad."

Tillman pulled the pot out before it finished dripping and began to swirl it around.

"Hey, you're making a mess over there, Tillman!" I told him. "The coffee hasn't finished dripping yet, man!"

"Hank'll clean it up. It's one of his chores for getting to live here for free." Tillman swished the coffee pot twelve times, poured some coffee in his mug, and then replaced the pot. He walked over to their double-door refrigerator, opened it, pulled out a pint of half-and-half, and filled the rest of his mug with it. I counted as he stirred the mug twelve times and tasted it. "Perfect," he said, smugly.

"Why do you do everything twelve times, Tillman?" I asked him, again.

"Twelve's my lucky number. My birthday's on the twelfth day of the twelfth month. December 12. Get it?"

"Wait a minute. You told me when we first met your birthday's in *November*. That's the *eleventh* month, Tillman."

"I did?"

"You sure did. 'Oh, what a tangled web we weave when first we practice to deceive.' "

"What's this supposed to mean?"

"It's what my Grandmother Justice always said

when she caught Billy or me in a lie."

"I wasn't lying. I have a photogenic memory."

"*Photographic*. Were too."

"Was not!"

"Were too."

"I *wasn't*, damn it! I've just got so much going on inside my brain…sometimes I get confused! They say geniuses do this a—"

"Liar."

"Redneck! Besides, it's not my fault. I'm obsessive-compulsive."

"What's that?"

"It's this very unique condition where you do the same thing over and over. All geniuses have it. At least, this is what my child psychologist says. And who's Billy? Is he your brother? Where is he? How old is he, and how come you haven't told me about him before?"

"You never asked me. But you'll get to meet him. He's driving down here today from Oxford in a truck. He's eighteen, and he just finished his freshman year at Ole Miss."

Hank walked into the kitchen smoking a cigarette. Hank wasn't wearing his ex-priest suit. He had on a pair of wrinkled khakis, a white, short-sleeved shirt with an old ink stain on it under the pocket, hippie sandals, and, of course, a black patch over his left eye. He looked only half-awake as he spoke to Tillman. "Sure do hope you made it strong this morning, Tillman. I stayed up too late last night. I'm getting too old to keep doing this, apparently." Then Hank looked at me. "Morning, for what it's worth."

"Mornin', Hank," I told him back.

"I didn't know you were up," Tillman said,

glancing at an antique kitchen clock on a wooden table in front of a window. "It's not even ten-thirty yet."

"I wasn't," Hank grumbled, "until somebody twisted the doorbell, *three damn times.*"

Hank looked at me sitting on the stool. "Let me guess. I bet it was…you?"

"Sorry, Hank."

"Forget it. Actually, I'm glad. I was having this dream I was a priest again, and I couldn't remember a single damn word of Latin. Weird… So why are you over here so early, Charlie?"

"That's what I asked him, too," Tillman added.

"Does everybody sleep so late in Natchez?" I asked.

"This isn't late, Charlie," Hank said. "Hell, most folks down in New Orleans don't wake up before twelve-thirty." Hank walked over to the sink, turned on the faucet, put out his smoke, and stuffed it down the drain. He rinsed a dirty New Orleans Saints mug from the sink and poured himself some coffee. Hank liked it black. "Not bad, Tillman," he said. "Much stronger this morning. Thank you."

"You're welcome, Hank—quite a compliment, coming from a gourmet chef from New Orleans." Tillman winked at me a third time. I wanted to knock one of his eyes out, too.

"I'm not a gourmet chef from New Orleans, Tillman. Like I've told you before, I'm just an ex-priest who used to teach English literature and philosophy to rich, Catholic, high school kids down there." Hank eyed the bag of chocolate cookies on top of the table in front of me. "I presume you have another request of the spirits, or should I say, *requests?*"

"No, just one," I told him.

"Then what's the whole bag for?"

"I didn't have another Hershey bar. Sorry."

"Yes, me too. So what's the request? Let's hear it."

"Right now?"

"Sure, why not? I'll pass it on to Tillie when she gets back. By the way, the spirits will probably want to know what kind of chocolate cookies you brought. What brand are they?"

"A&P."

"Oh. Well, I hope it's not a big request. I'm not sure if they like this brand or not."

"Sorry. It's all we had."

"Figures," Tillman said. Tillman walked over with his mug of coffee and sat down on the stool next to me. "Yeah, Hall, what's your new request—for your ol' man?"

"This one is for your father, Charlie?" Hank wrinkled his brow at me.

"Yes, sir," I told him.

"Is he aware you came over here to make a request of the spirits for him?"

"No, sir."

"It's gratuitous, then?"

"Sir?" I didn't understand what Hank meant by this.

"Gratuitous, Hall," Tillman stated. "It means you're doing this for your ol' man for free."

"Wrong, Tillman," Hank noted. "It means Charlie is doing this for his father out of *love*. There is nothing free, my lads, not even life itself." Hank took a gulp of the coffee and patted his shirt pocket for another smoke. "Tillman, I left my cigarettes upstairs. They're on the nightstand next to my bed. How about retrieving them for me, please? Tillman? Did you hear—"

"Huh?" Tillman was leaned over on his stool, picking at one of his disgusting toenails. "What'd you say?"

"I said, eschew this execrable toe procedure you're doing, get your stinky butt up, and go grab my cigarettes. *Now!*"

Tillman gave Hank a glad grin and hopped off the stool. "Sure, Hank, no problemo! Be glad to! Be right back!" He shot out of the kitchen and ran into the hall. Then I heard Tillman slip and fall. He yelled out loud, like Tillie, "Damn this old runner!"

"No hurry, Tillman. Please, take your time. And don't you smoke any! I know how many Marlboros I have left in the pack—I counted!" Hank bellowed toward the hall.

"Don't worry, I won't!" Tillman hollered back. I heard Tillman run down the hall and quickly walk up the long flight of stairs, two steps at a time, like Rhett Butler did.

Hank walked over to the table and sat down on the stool Tillman had been sitting on, next to me. "Now we can talk in privacy. He'll be up there for at least five minutes smoking one of my cigarettes. Maybe two of them." Hank reached over and picked up the bag of A&P chocolate cookies. "Mind if I partake of some?"

"No, help yourself."

Hank ripped open the bag and tossed a couple cookies into his mouth. "Not bad," Hank mumbled. He washed them down with coffee. "Okay. Let's hear your request, Charlie, for your father. The spirits are curious."

I cleared my throat. "Well, what I want is, I mean, what I want for my *dad* is…I want him to make a lot of money in his new job." I looked at Hank. "This is all I'm asking."

"You know, this A&P brand is quite tasty." Hank got a third cookie from the bag and started eating it. "I'll have to tell Tillie to buy some the next time she goes shopping. It's where she is right now. The A&P. Tuesday morning's when she always goes. Fewer people then." He ate a fourth cookie, and then he proceeded to eat a fifth one.

"Well?" I said. Hank seemed oblivious to what I had just asked.

"Well, what?"

"Did you hear what I just asked the spirits to do for my dad?"

"Of course I heard you," Hank said as he swallowed his fifth cookie. "I may be half-blind, but I'm not deaf. They heard you, too. I'm trying to listen to what they're saying while I eat. They're still considering your request."

"Oh. Good. Just wanted to make sure."

"Shhh… I can barely hear them. They're mumbling. They're still sleepy, too."

"Sorry."

Hank nodded his head, two or three times, as if the spirits were telling him something. He said, " 'Before they call, I will answer. While they are still speaking, I will hear…' "

"What in the world…?"

"Isaiah 65, verse 24, Protestant version. Have you ever read the Bible, Charlie?"

I was embarrassed to have to answer Hank. "Yes.

Well…no. Mother has, though, lots of times. She used to read it to me and Billy and Sis all the time, before…before Sis—"

"Yes, I know, Charlie. Tillie already told me. She had one of her spirit dreams last night, and they showed her everything that happened to y'all up in Tupelo. *Everything.* I'm sorry. I understand better, now."

"What'd Tillie tell you, Hank? Understand *what* better? I'm not following you."

"Charlie, we have a slight dilemma here," Hank said, changing the subject. "As I just quoted from the mightiest of all the ancient prophets, Isaiah, the spirits have heard you, and they do desire to oblige you, but your existing gift is much too—how shall I say this— 'paltry,' for such a huge request."

"What does that mean?"

"In the vernacular…the cookies don't cut it."

"I don't understand. I thought they liked chocolate."

"They do, dear boy, they assuredly do." Hank shoved the bag of cookies back in front of me. "And they said to thank you, most profusely. But a request of this magnitude will require a major gift. We don't want to offend the spirits."

"No, we definitely don't. Nope, not me. I hate toads and stray cats."

"So what else can you offer them?"

"I ain't got nothin' else. I really don't know what I can offer them, Hank. What do you think they want?"

"I don't know, Charlie. So I would propose, again, we let them decide what your second gift should be. Ready?"

"This means to shut up again, right?"

"Right." Just as he had done out on the front porch the night before, Hank closed his right eye, folded both his arms in front of him, and bowed his head. He started chanting the same song again, and, as I sat there on the stool staring at him, he reminded me of this Buddha statue I had once seen in one of Dad's *National Geographic* magazines. It was fat and bald too, but this Buddha had *two* eyes, and I doubted it was Catholic.

This time, it didn't take Hank long to get the word. He raised his head, opened his right eye, and stuck his arms out in front of him, palms up. "Something is found, something old, something round, something gold." Hank looked over at me and said, "Well, there you have it."

"Have what?"

"What I just revealed from the spirits…what they want from you for their second gift."

"But I don't understand what you said. It sounded like some sort of riddle to me."

"That's because it is. Most things in life usually are. We're seldom led straight into the Promised Land, Charlie. God wants to develop our faith *and* our brains. This is one of the main reasons Jesus spoke in parables. Do you understand what I'm trying to tell you here, son?"

"No, not really."

"Well, you're not alone, because I frankly don't either. Anyway, let's try to figure this thing out together. Okay?"

"Okay, thanks, but what do you think the spirits meant by 'something is found?' "

"To me, it sounds like the spirits have probably lost something, and if you can find it, then this will be your second gift to them."

"How can I find something when I don't even know what it *is*, or where to start looking?"

"They've already told you what it is. It's old, round, and gold."

"But where'd they lose it? There's so much junk—I mean, *stuff*—in this old mansion, I wouldn't know where to—"

"No, junk is right. *Old* junk is probably even better. And it's just an old house, Charlie, not a mansion. But as to where to start looking, well, I'm afraid I can't help you there. You'll have to figure this one out on your own."

"But, but—"

"No more 'buts,' Charlie. Just *believe* you will find your second gift, and you will. It's just that simple." Hank took the last swallow of coffee from his mug, then yawned and stretched.

"I better go upstairs and check on Tillman. The little reiver's probably on his second or third cigarette by now."

Hank stood up from his stool. I never saw him do it, but I realized later Hank had probably reached inside the pocket of his pants, pulled out a small gold coin, and quickly placed it on top of his stool before he stood.

Hank set his coffee mug down. "I swear on my ex-priest's honor I'm going to wring Tillman's scrawny neck if he's hiding in my closet again, smoking. He'd better be on the back porch up there. There's plenty of orange juice in the refrigerator, Charlie, if you'd like some, since apparently you don't drink coffee. Be right back. Start looking." Then Hank left.

I got up from my stool and walked across the

kitchen to the biggest refrigerator I had ever seen. I opened one of the two doors. It was crammed full of food, beverages, wine, and various condiments, just like every room in their home was with, as Hank and I now agreed, "old junk."

I saw a plastic jug of orange juice in the back of the refrigerator and grabbed it. I started to remove the cap and take a swig, but I figured this was probably what Tillman did, too, so I decided to use a glass. I got a clean one from a cabinet, filled it, and put the jug back inside the refrigerator. I walked over to my stool to sit down, drink my juice, and try to decide where to start looking for this old, round, gold thing the spirits had apparently lost…

And that is when I spotted it.

Lying there on top of the stool where Hank had been sitting was a gold coin about the size of a dime. At first, I couldn't believe my eyes. *What the…?* I picked up the coin and examined it. It had the engraved face of an Indian wearing a huge headdress on the front of it, with the year "1929" stamped below it, and the word "Liberty" stamped on top.

The Tupelo redneck in me then reared its ugly head. *Hey, this looks like real gold. It's round, it's old, and I just found it. This must be it!* I was amazed, not just at my brains but also at my good luck. *I can't believe it! This is it; it has to be! This is what the spirits must have lost, and I just found it!* "Hank, Hank…!" I began to holler, as loud as I could. "I found it! I just found it, Hank! Come see! Come see…!"

Hank hollered back from the top of the stairs. "Hold on down there—I'm coming! What'd you just find?" I heard Hank and Tillman walking down the stairs together.

"You're not gonna believe it!" I was too excited to wait until Hank made it into the kitchen, so I ran out with the coin in my hand. I ran down the hall toward the stairs, without tripping, and met Hank just as he stepped onto the bottom step. Tillman was standing behind him. "Look, Hank!" I stuck my right hand out and proudly showed them both what I had just found. "It's old, round, and, I think, real gold! This must be what the spirits lost! And it was right there on your stool! I saw it after you got up and left the kitchen! I can't believe it, can you?"

Hank squinted his eye and took the coin out of my palm. "Well, now, let's just have a closer look at this thing…"

Tillman peered over Hank's shoulder and raised his red eyebrows. Even though he was chewing a big wad of gum, his breath still reeked of cigarettes. "Hey, Hank, that's Tillie's old—"

"Cease and desist, Tillman. Cease and desist. Never squash another person's belief."

"I'm going back upstairs," Tillman said. He turned and started to walk up the steps. "I've gotta go take a you-know-what. Later, Hall," he said as he left.

"Yeah, later, Tillman. See ya. Do you really believe this is what the spirits lost, Hank? Do you?"

Hank held the coin up to the ceiling light in the hall and examined it. "It definitely looks and feels like real gold to me, but there's only one way to be sure." Hank put the coin between his teeth and bit down on it. "Yep, it's real gold, all right."

"How can you tell by biting on it?"

"I don't really know, but it's what they always do

in those old westerns on TV."

"So you think this old coin is what the spirits lost?"

"I'm positive it is. No doubt about it."

"This is my second gift to them, right? And now my second request, for my dad, will be granted. Right, Hank?"

"Right, Charlie. Your dad's going to get it."

"You'll give the spirits the coin, won't you?"

"I wouldn't dare not to."

"I still can't believe it, though, Hank. Can you?"

Hank flipped the five-dollar gold piece in the air and caught it in his hand. "Why, of course I can, Charlie. Like I told you last night and again this morning…believing is what it's all about."

I left Hank standing in the hall with the gold coin in his hand, and Tillman sitting on one of the two commodes upstairs, and I ran out of their house, about ten-thirty Tuesday morning.

I was on top of the world and still couldn't believe my good fortune! I jumped down the last three front steps onto the ground, without even falling. I was positive I would never fall nor fail again—not for the rest of my life! *How could I?* I had to be special, blessed by both God and Tillie's spirit friends, whoever or whatever they were. But at the moment, it really didn't matter.

When I looked across the street and saw a white van in our driveway with Natchez Cable TV Company printed on the back of it, I checked for traffic, ran across Melrose Avenue, and caught the cable guy on our front porch just as he was preparing to knock on the red door. "It's locked," I told him. "Stay here. I'll go around the back and let you in."

I couldn't wait for Billy to arrive. I knew he wouldn't believe it all, but there was so much I wanted to tell him. As I ran around the house, I had no doubt. This was going to be the most memorable day of my life.

I was definitely correct.

Chapter Eleven

We assumed Billy left Ole Miss a little after six Tuesday morning and drove over to Tupelo. I'm sure he forgot to call Grandmother and let her know he would be coming, but he probably figured this was best. Grandmother would have called Mother, and Mother would have told her to tell Billy to come home immediately, like she had ordered him.

Grandmother told us Billy knocked on her screen door about seven-thirty, and she couldn't believe her eyes. "Why, Billy," she said, "what a pleasant surprise! I thought you were on your way down to Natchez today."

"I am, Gramma, but I wanted to visit you first."

"Well, then come on in. I was just having my oatmeal and dry toast."

I know Grandmother Justice was happy to see Billy, but she would have never told him so. She was just like Mother. I don't remember my Grandfather Justice at all. He died when I was only two. Dad confided to me once, though, that Grandfather Justice was an "abusive alcoholic" and that "the Scotch finally killed him."

I simply assumed Dad meant Grandfather used to get drunk and fight the McCranies. They lived across the street from Grandmother and him. The McCranies were the only "Scotch" family I knew in Tupelo, and

Mr. McCranie used to wear a green-and-red plaid skirt around all the time. One Sunday morning, he even wore it to the Presbyterian church. Some of the people laughed, but not me. I couldn't believe a grown man would actually wear a *skirt* to church. So I never blamed my grandfather for fighting the McCranies, even though I believed they had killed him. I wanted to kill Mr. McCranie that Sunday morning, too, and for an entire year after this. Like too many revelations in life, though, I later learned what my dad had meant and what I had merely assumed, as a child, were two different matters.

After Billy had eaten a bowl of oatmeal and a piece of dry toast with Grandmother, he drove her in her Mary Kay pink Cadillac to the Tupelo City Cemetery to see Sis's grave. It was still there. They stayed and talked to her bones for about ten minutes, and then Grandmother Justice said she started complaining about the summer heat, the mosquitoes, and how all the lazy city workers never kept the graves cut, so she told Billy to take her back home. Before they left, Billy asked Grandmother if she wanted to go visit Grandfather Justice's grave, on the other side of the cemetery. "No," she told Billy. "That's why I buried him over there. Let's go."

Billy took Grandmother back home to her brick bungalow at 23 Lee Street, and they went inside and drank some iced tea. They talked about Natchez, and Grandmother warned Billy most folks there were Catholic and peculiar, so he had best be circumspect.

Before Billy kissed Grandmother goodbye, he told her not to worry about him and he'd always look after me, no matter what. Grandmother said she worried, though. She told us she sensed something about Billy seemed different.

Grandmother said Billy left her house about ten. He probably stopped at a convenience store, bought a pack of Winstons and a six-pack of Budweiser, iced it down, and then called his friend, Benny Kidd. Benny was never interested in college, but he could shoot pool better than any guy I knew, so he was always one of my heroes, growing up. That day in the parlor, later, Benny told us he and Billy met at eleven, and then they hooked up with Ron Norris and his new girlfriend, and the four of them went to get a burger at Nellie's Place, in the black part of town.

Benny said Billy talked a lot about Ann Marie and told them all about the fight and his getting kicked out of Ole Miss, but he said none of them were really surprised to hear it.

It was past one-thirty when Billy finally told them all goodbye, got in his car, and headed south to Natchez, Benny added.

Billy probably knew that Mother would be making dinner, that he'd be running late, and that he probably should call from a pay phone and let her know, but he never did.

Billy was just like my dad.

****

I don't believe Mother and Tillie both going to the A&P the same morning was coincidental because I don't believe in coincidences, anymore. I've grown to believe in miracles. It had to be a miracle Tillie told my mother the real truth that Tuesday morning in May of 1978, the day that changed my mother's life. The day that changed *all* our lives, forever.

This is what Mother told my dad and me later, after Dad finally got home:

Mother was in the checkout line with hamburger meat, noodles, and whatever it takes to make spaghetti sauce, plus a lot of other things we needed around the house. There was an older, black lady standing in front of Mother, buying some menthol snuff and paying for it with a handful of coins. When the checkout girl told the black lady she didn't have enough money to pay for the snuff, a white woman's hand reached around Mother and handed the black lady a ten-dollar bill. The black lady turned around and recognized the white woman and said, "Praise the Lord, Mrs. Dawes—you sure is one fine Christian soul! I sure do thank you. Yes'm, I do."

"Glad I can help, Cora. You keep the rest of the change."

"Lord love you, dear," Cora said. "Thank you, Jesus!"

When Mother turned around and saw it was Tillie who had helped the black lady, she said she was embarrassed. Mother said she quickly turned back and prayed Tillie hadn't recognized her.

Tillie did, though, and she tapped Mother on her shoulder. "Excuse me," Tillie said nicely, "but aren't you Mrs. Hall, Charlie's mother?"

Mother said she was speechless, at first, but then she slowly turned again and said, "Why, yes, I am. And you're Mrs. Dawes, correct? From across the street. You have such a lovely, antebellum home. It must be nice to—"

"Thank you," Tillie said, "but it's really a mess inside. And it needs painting, I know. It just costs so much to—"

"No," Mother said she told Tillie, "it's exquisite. I...I've never seen such a beautiful house in my entire life."

"Well, they're all over Natchez. If anything, it's the problem with this town—too many old homes and old people around, like me. Not enough new houses and young folks here."

"I'm sorry I didn't recognize you at first, Mrs. Dawes. You just look so, so *different* than when I first met you yesterday evening."

"Yes, I'm out of uniform, you could say. I generally hear this when I dress in pants and flats and happen to bump into a client somewhere."

Mother began unloading her groceries onto the counter. "*Client*? I didn't know you were some sort of 'professional.' What exactly do you do, Mrs. Dawes? By the way, it was a very nice gesture you just did for that poor black woman."

"*Black lady*. Thank you. This is what I do...I help people."

"Excuse me?"

"I said I help people, Mrs. Hall."

"Oh? Well, it's apparent you are quite generous, and please call me 'Claire.' "

"Thank you, Claire. And you please call me 'Tillie.' I'm really not generous, though. I charge for my services."

Mother lifted the three-pound package of hamburger meat and put it on the counter. "And just exactly what are your 'services,' Tillie, if you don't mind my asking?"

"Of course not, Claire, not at all. I help people

see."

"See? See what?" Mother said she raised her eyebrows at Tillie.

"The truth."

"*The truth*? How interesting." Mother smirked. Then she turned and looked at the checkout girl. "I believe the hamburger meat is on sale. Did you ring it up correctly?"

"Yes, ma'am," she said, "it is. I rang it up right."

Mother said she was now more convinced than ever that Tillie Dawes was not only incorrigible but also insane. *The truth. No wonder Tillman is so disturbed*, she told us she thought. But as she removed the loaf of French bread from the cart and put it on the counter, Mother said something told her to talk to Tillie again. "I do hope my Charlie wasn't bothering you last night, Mrs. Dawes?"

"Tillie."

"Tillie, sorry. I assure you, though, it won't happen again."

"Not in the least, Claire. Frankly, I think Charlie is a wonderful young man. He's always welcome to come visit us at any time. Day or night."

"Possibly you didn't understand me, Tillie?" Mother said she looked Tillie Dawes in her eyes. "Charlie will never be visiting your home again. I've forbidden him from doing so, and he's grounded for doing it last night."

"Yes, I know this, Claire, but I told him it was okay."

"This all comes to $34.97, please, ma'am," the young checkout girl told my mother.

"I beg your pardon?" Mother said she couldn't

believe her ears.

"I said, your total is thirty-four dollars and—"

"No, not you, I heard what you just said!" Mother said she was shaking with indignation as she reached inside her purse. She unzipped her billfold and quickly handed the girl two twenty-dollar bills. "Here, and I *do* collect green stamps!" Mother glared at Tillie. "What did you just say?"

"I said, I told Charlie it was okay, and not to—"

"How *dare* you tell my son to disobey me when I order him—"

"And not to cry anymore, because you really don't hate him, you just never learned how to love him. Just like your mother never learned how to love you. It's not your fault, Claire. It never has been. It wasn't your mother's fault, either. I'm sorry she never told you this, but you mustn't blame her anymore. She never knew any better. No one ever told her so, like I'm telling you now."

Mother told us the checkout girl seemed afraid to interrupt. "Uh, here's your change, ma'am…your green stamps, too."

My mother said she could barely speak. Without ever looking away from Tillie's eyes, she somehow managed to say, "No. You, you keep, you just keep it, okay? The stamps, too…"

"Thank you, ma'am! I'll bag your things for you now."

Mother stared in disbelief at Tillie Dawes. She told us she was mesmerized by her, paralyzed by a plethora of emotions—shock, remorse, grief, and an overwhelming fear it was too late for her to change. She said she had never heard or encountered such insight, such wisdom before. Mother felt naked, exposed, vulnerable…human, for the first time in her life. She said she didn't know whether to curse or to cry. But the more she peered into Tillie's dark brown eyes, the more she saw compassion, understanding, forgiveness, acceptance, and most importantly…freedom.

"Your things are all bagged, ma'am," the girl finally told her.

Mother didn't respond. She was afraid to look away from Tillie, afraid to lose what she said she had always desired and needed the most. An honest friend.

"Ma'am," the girl said to my mother, "are you okay?"

Mother said she was waging a desperate battle inside to not lose control, to not let go, to not break down and cry.

I didn't know it then, but Mother told us she had never in her life cried before, not even when she was young, not even when Sis died. She had never learned how to.

"Ma'am," the checkout girl said again, "I need to ask you to please get your bags now. They're in the cart. Other customers are waiting in line behind you."

Mother said her hand was surprisingly steady as she reached up and gently felt the right side of Tillie's face. Though her skin was taut, it was also warm and, mainly, real. Tillie wasn't an angel, as Mother had first imagined when Tillie told her the *real* truth, that morning.

Tillie took Mother's hand and placed it between hers. "It's okay, Claire. It's okay to go home now. Go home to Charlie and tell him you love him. And tell him I said hello."

****

Dad said he was sitting at his desk going through some files when his telephone intercom buzzed, about three o'clock Tuesday afternoon. "Yes, Evelyn?" he answered, assuming it was probably his secretary. "Oh, hey, Ed, I didn't know it was you… Sure, I'll be right in. Do I need to bring any of my files with me? Okay. I'm on my way."

Dad hung up the phone, and he said he got this unsettling thought Ed didn't sound like his usual jovial self. He sounded strangely somber, formal. It bothered him, he told us. Dad got his blazer from the metal coat stand and put it on, straightened his tie, and walked out of his office. He nodded to Evelyn, who was sitting at her desk, typing an auto claim report. Dad had only known Evelyn for less than two days, but he said he sensed Evelyn was astute, so she could probably tell something was going on; the look on her face gave him that impression.

Dad walked up the carpeted hall, slower than his usual pace, toward Ed's office at the very front of the building. The polished brass nameplate on the wall next to Ed's door read: Edgar L. Radford, Jr., President. The door was shut tight. Dad said he started to knock but hesitated. He took a couple of deep breaths to settle his nerves, and then he softly knocked three times on the opaque-glass panel on the top half of the door. From inside, Ed told Dad to come in.

Ed's office was plush, formal, intimidating, and at least two times larger than Dad's. Ed was seated in a tall, black-leather recliner behind a mahogany partner's desk, which had once belonged to his father. There were diplomas, family pictures, and years of acquired memorabilia all over the huge office. Directly behind Ed, on the wall over his credenza, was his most prized possession, according to Dad: a framed, Ole Miss football jersey with a red "18" on it, personally autographed: To my favorite fan, Ed Radford, Jr. Signed, Archie Manning.

Ed was a huge Rebel fan. He detested Mississippi State and Alabama, and he regularly cursed LSU, according to my father.

Dad slowly walked inside. Ed's arms were folded on the writing mat in front of him. He was leaning forward, and a frown was on his face. Ed removed his thick, black glasses and set them to the right side of the mat, next to his Ole Miss Rebel coffee mug. Very matter-of-factly, Ed asked my dad to shut the door and to please have a seat in the left chair in front of his desk.

Sitting in the right chair in front of Ed's desk was a man about five years younger than Dad. My dad said he didn't recognize him at first, but after he sat down and glanced over at him, he immediately knew who he was. They nodded their heads at each other in recognition, but Dad said neither he nor the other man spoke to each other or smiled.

After several seconds of painful silence, Ed pointed at the other man and said, "William, I believe you know Jon, here?"

"Yes," Dad said, "we met briefly on my second interview." Dad extended his right hand and spoke to Jon Wilson. "Good to see you again, Jon. How goes it?"

"Good, William," Jon said. "Very good, in fact. Sorry I haven't stopped by your office yet. I just got back into town, about two. Been up in Jackson since Friday."

"No problem, Jon," Dad replied. "We'll have lunch one day this week, okay?"

Dad said Jon didn't say a word back to him. Instead, Jon turned and looked at Ed.

Ed cleared his throat. He picked up his glasses and put them back on. "Uh, William, this probably won't be possible. Frankly, it's what we wanted to discuss with you today."

Dad tried to loosen his tight collar. "Sure, Ed. Sorry to hear this, though, Jon. I hope nothing's wrong?"

"No, William. I'm fine. How's your family doing? If I recall, you have two sons. Correct?"

"Right. Billy and Charlie. They're both fine. Thanks for asking."

"You haven't bought a house here yet, have you?" Dad said Jon asked him next.

"Uh, no. No. We, we decided to just rent first. It's close to Charlie's school. He can ride his new bike there. And, well, you know how it is, Jon. Till we see…see how things go…where the best neighborhoods are, those kinds of—"

"Trust me, William, I do understand." Dad said Jon reached over and touched his right sleeve with his left hand.

Ed cleared his throat again. He took his glasses off and gestured with them, like Gregory Peck did in that big courtroom scene in *To Kill a Mockingbird*, Dad told us. "Let's get down to business, gentlemen. Okay?" Ed said. "I'm afraid we have a pressing situation on our hands. But before I tell you why I called you into my office, William, I first want to say…"

Ed proceeded to advise my father that Jon Wilson had been with the agency for only two years, but he had already made vice-president and was one of their most respected and diligent employees. Jon's face flushed. He seemed to be truly humbled by Ed's praise, Dad told us all, and Jon thanked Ed.

Ed then informed Dad that, in addition to handling most of their auto accident claims, Jon was a former policeman, so he managed all their adjustors and outside investigators. "As a matter of fact," Ed said, "one of our investigators is from Tupelo, William, and he told Jon he knew you. Knew you well. What's his name again, Jon?" Ed asked.

"Gerald Hamilton. Used to be a policeman, too, before he became an insurance claims investigator. We graduated from the State Academy together, twenty years ago. Wow, I was only eighteen then. It's hard to believe it's been this long, you know?"

Dad tried to unbutton his collar. He tried to swallow. "Yeah, Jon, I…I know what you mean. Time flies when you're having fun, huh?" Dad said he smiled, nervously, but he probably looked like a shifty crook who had just been brought in for questioning.

"Anyway… Right, that's his name, Gerald Hamilton. Does excellent work. Very thorough. I assume you know him, William?" Ed asked.

Dad said he slid down in his chair, finally undid the button of his collar, and loosened his tie. "Uh, yeah, Ed, yeah, I know Gerald. A fine fellow. We used to go to church together in Tupelo. First Presbyterian. Our oldest sons played—"

"Notwithstanding, William," Ed leaned back and

said, "Jon called me from Jackson yesterday morning and informed me of something, well, I rather suspected. And it concerns you. I started to discuss this with you yesterday afternoon, before you went home, but I wanted Jon to be here when I did so. And, frankly, I wanted to sleep on it last night. And pray about it, too. I believe in prayer, men—always have, always will. It's the only thing that got me through all the horrible shelling from those Germans at Bastogne during World War II. And that Christmas in Belgium, 1944—hell, I've never been as cold in my life! Damn near froze to death.

"I also wanted to discuss this with Jon, face to face, first. It's a major decision about to be made today. But after talking with Jon the past hour, William, I know—we *both* know—it's the right decision to make…"

Dad told us he walked out of Ed's office shortly after four o'clock with a stunned look on his face. He also said he was glad Ed's old blue-blood secretary wasn't sitting in her office at her desk. And he told us he especially didn't want to see Evelyn or Jerry or anyone else, at this particular moment.

So he walked quickly down the hall without speaking to anyone he passed and headed straight for the men's room. He walked inside and checked under all three stalls to ensure he was completely alone. He said he walked over to one of the three sinks and just stared at himself in the mirror for several seconds. He stood there shaking his head in total amazement, barely believing what Edgar L. Radford, Junior had just told him.

"I can't believe it. I simply can't believe it," my dad said he told his reflection in the mirror. "I don't deserve this, Lord. You *know* I don't. Why should this happen to me? Why…?"

He told Mother he thought about calling her immediately and telling her what had happened. Instead, Dad decided to just leave and go home. This way, he could avoid seeing Evelyn and Jerry and the rest of the twelve employees who worked there. Besides, he said to us, they would all hear the news, soon enough.

And he wanted to tell my mother when they were both sitting down. Together.

Chapter Twelve

It was almost three o'clock when Mother finally opened the front door and walked into the house, and I could tell immediately something was wrong with her, big time. In fact, I don't remember ever seeing her look this way before.

I first had this crazy thought she looked like she was drunk. After all, she *was* two hours late and had spaghetti and meatballs to make before Billy got home in a couple of hours. I couldn't possibly imagine what Mother had been doing all afternoon. So when Grandpa Hall's Seth Thomas clock had tolled twice, an hour earlier, I began to worry.

But I knew Mother had never had a drink in her forty-two years of pious, pharisaic living, so I dismissed this notion. I was curious, though, where she had been.

"So where you been, Mother? I was startin' to worry."

Mother was standing at the door with a strange smile on her face. "Oh, I'm so sorry, Charlie. I should have called I'd be late. Please forgive me." She had two full A&P bags in her arms, and she tried to maneuver the bag in her left arm to check the time on her watch. "It's three o'clock already? I can't fathom I've been gone this long. Billy might get here early, and I haven't even started on the sauce yet... Charlie, I hate to ask you this, but I'm really going to need your help, okay?"

"Sure, whatever." The grandfather clock in the den chimed three times. I hopped up from the sofa. "Just let me know what to do. I don't mind, really. Are there some more things in the station wagon you want me to bring in?"

"Yes. There're two more big bags out there. Would you, please?" Mother saw the TV was on. "Good, the cable company finally came today. I'm glad."

"Yeah, me too. Do you need me to help you with those?"

"No. These are both light. I can get them... Charlie?"

"Yes, ma'am?"

"I went by and visited the First Presbyterian Church in downtown Natchez after lunch. It's directly across from City Hall. I spent some time in there, just thinking and praying. I thanked God for giving us a safe trip down here and for your dad's new job. It's a magnificent church, and it's old, very old. I think we'll like it there. Who knows, maybe your dad might even start going with us again."

Your dad? I had never heard Mother refer to him as "dad" before. Ever. For all my life it had always been "your father." I was totally confused by this obvious, dramatic change which had occurred in my mother since she left our house that morning. Something had come over her or happened to her, but I couldn't figure what it could possibly be.

The third surprise of my day was about to come, and there would be three more to follow.

"Oh, I saw Tillie Dawes at the A&P this morning when I was checking out. She said you were a 'wonderful young man' and to be sure to tell you hello.

You know something, son? I don't believe I've ever met anyone quite like her before. Not in my whole life. And I have the strangest feeling she and I are going to become close friends."

"Uh, I better go get those other two bags now," I said quickly.

As I started to leave, Mother asked me, "Has Billy called yet?"

"No, ma'am, but Grandmother called about twelve-thirty. She said Billy stopped by there this morning and had oatmeal and dry toast with her. Then he took her out to the cemetery to see Sis's grave. Grandmother said he left her house about ten."

"Good. It was very considerate of Billy to go see her first. I know she appreciated this."

My mother glanced at her watch again. "You know, I bet he stopped off and saw a few of his old friends, too. You know Billy. And they probably all had lunch somewhere…" She seemed to be talking to herself next. "Good. This should give me till five-thirty before Billy—"

"She said to tell you to call her, too, just as soon as you got home."

"What?" Mother seemed to not have heard me.

"Grandmother Justice."

"Oh, well…we'll call her tonight, after we all eat. I have to get dinner started first."

"I fed the baby mockingbird this morning. It, uh, was flying all around in its box. I bet it can probably—"

"I'm glad you reminded me. Thanks for doing this, son."

Mother walked across the den. I was standing next to the coffee table. She put both of her bags down on the sofa and bent down in front of me. She put her hands on my arms. "Would you do one other thing for me, Charlie? I think it's time we let the baby bird go. I shouldn't ever have caged it in a box. I was just afraid some cat might try to kill it, that's all. So take it outside and let it go for me. Okay? It's big enough to fly away and live on its own now."

Mother had tears in her eyes. I swallowed a lump in my throat as big as a walnut.

"Mother, what's the matter? Why are you crying? Mother? What's wrong? Mom…?"

She didn't even try to hold back the tears. Her lips were quivering as she looked into my eyes. She was so close to me I could smell the rouge on her face.

"Charlie, Charlie, can you ever find it in your heart to forgive me? I've been so wrong. Please believe I *do* love you. I've *always* loved you and Billy both. I…I just, just…" Mother grabbed me and hugged me, and I hugged her back. I laid my head on the left shoulder of her dress and probably stained it from all the tears which fell from my own eyes, down her back. I didn't care, though, and neither did she.

Mother hugged me tightly, backed up a bit, and looked me in the face. Neither of us was embarrassed or the least bit ashamed, and it was probably the truest moment of both our lives. We both wiped our noses and eyes with the back of our hands. Mother stood up and looked at me. "Charlie, I know you probably think I've lost my senses. But the truth is, son—I've finally just *come* to them."

I knew I should be as honest with my mother as she was being with me, but all I could say was, "I agree with you about that baby bird. I'm sure it can fly now."

"Well, do this for me later. First, run get those bags from the car so I can get dinner started. I've got to hurry."

****

I was in the kitchen, rinsing off a head of lettuce to make the salad with, and my mother was tasting the spaghetti sauce from the pot with her wooden spoon, when Dad walked in the front door, about four-thirty. He hung his blazer on the coat rack and slowly closed the door behind him. As he came into the den, he noticed the television was finally on, and Dad stood there for a few moments watching Gomer Pyle hollering, "Citizen's arrest! Citizen's arrest!" at Deputy Barney Fife as Barney made an unlawful U-turn in Sheriff Andy Taylor's patrol car on the only street in Mayberry, North Carolina.

Dad walked into the kitchen. He was quiet and still, like he was a ghost, watching us. Mother finally turned around and saw him, and it startled her so much she dropped her spoon on the floor. "William, you almost scared me to death!" She looked up at the clock over the stove. "It's only four-thirty-five. What are you doing home so early?"

"Hey, Dad," I smiled and said. "The TV's working now."

"Yeah. I really like Andy Griffith." He glanced back toward the den. "This episode always makes me laugh."

But Dad didn't look like he had been laughing, to me.

Mother picked the spoon off the floor. "Are you feeling okay, William? You're not sick, are you? Can I get you an—"

"No. I'm fine. Really. Has Billy called yet?"

"No, not yet. He should be here in about an hour, though." Mother wiped the spaghetti sauce from the floor with a wet paper towel, then rinsed off the spoon in the sink.

"Okay. Well, I think I'll go take a bath, then. I, uh, I just need to be alone for a while, Claire. I hope you don't mind. Is there anything you need me to do first?"

"No, not really. Charlie's been helping me around the house since I got home. He got his room ready for Billy to stay in. And he even cleaned off the back porch. I figure Billy can put his things out there, at least till we decide if he should stay here for the summer or not."

"Good. I'm going to draw my bath water now."

"William," Mother asked again, "are you sure you're not—"

"I'm fine, Claire. I promise. I just have a lot on my mind, right now. Please don't worry, okay?" Dad began to take off his tie as he walked from the kitchen into the dining room.

As he walked to their bedroom at the end of the hall, I looked at Mother. "I didn't know Dad liked baths," I said to her.

"He doesn't, and he hates the Andy Griffith show...*especially* Gomer Pyle. I wish I knew what was going on. He just seems so, so...different. Distant, too. I hope nothing bad happened at work today," she said to me.

****

At ten minutes past six, the three of us were sitting at the dinner table and still waiting on Billy to get home. We hadn't started eating yet because Mother said we absolutely couldn't begin without him.

Mother didn't have time to make the cheesecake she had bought the ingredients for, so she suggested to Dad we all go to the Malt Shack after dinner for some ice cream. She told Dad she had seen it when she was coming home, and it just had to be better than Burger Chef. Of course, I agreed. Then Mother told him about the Presbyterian church downtown, how beautiful, serene, and old it was, and how she had prayed for our family while she was in there.

I assumed Mother was about to ask Dad if he would consider going to church with us again, but instead, she told him about meeting Tillie at the A&P grocery store that morning. I listened intently as Mother revealed what Tillie had said to her and how certain she was God had just sent her a friend.

Dad was conciliatory, but he looked distracted, disinterested. He nodded a few times as Mother told her cathartic story, but he never said a single word. He was merely an empty suit in an empty chair.

This was unusual for him not to speak, especially since Mother was being so open and friendly. I had no idea what was going on, but when I looked over at Mother and realized Dad's bizarre mood was killing her new spirit, I finally decided enough was enough. I had to try to snap him out of whatever kind of funk he was in.

"Dad, will you *please* say something back to Mom? Can't you see how hard she's trying to be—"

"The spaghetti's getting cold, and Billy is apparently running late," was all he said.

Mother bit her lips to keep from crying. "Yes, William, you're right. We might as well start without him. I'll warm Billy a plate when he gets here."

"Do you mind if I bless it first, Claire?"

Mother and I looked at each other in amazement.

"Absolutely, William." Mother said, "I think this would be wonderful. You…you haven't done this in—"

"I know, in way too long. Let's all join hands now and bow our heads." Dad proceeded to give thanks. When he finished, Mother and I started eating lukewarm spaghetti and meatballs.

Dad was just toying with his. "Is it not warm enough for you, William? I'll be happy to take your plate and heat it in the oven."

Without looking up, Dad said, "No, it's fine. I'm just not very hungry. I'm still trying to figure it all out in my head, that's all."

"Figure what out, William?" Mother put her fork down. "What are you talking about?"

"What happened today at work. It just doesn't make any sense, Claire. None at all. I've only been there two days, for God's sake."

Mother turned white as my milk. I had never seen the abject face of terror before, but that's what I saw when I looked at her. I was scared myself, but I realize now my fear, when this happened, was born of naivety and ignorance. Mother's fear was born of familiarity, broken promises, shattered dreams, banished hope. She tried to speak, but she couldn't utter a word. I wanted to help my mother, but I didn't know how to. No one had ever taught me.

"Ed called me into his office today about three. Totally out of the blue," Dad announced, abruptly. "I didn't have a clue… Claire, do you remember me mentioning this Jon Wilson guy I met, the second time I drove down here to interview with Ed's agency?"

Mother slowly shook her head.

"Well, I didn't really care for Jon. He's probably four or five years younger than me, I'd say. Formal, aloof, not really a bad sort, just someone I didn't feel comfortable around. Anyway, I found out today from Ed that Jon's a former cop, and wouldn't you just know it, he and Gerald Hamilton from Tupelo are old friends. You remember Gerald, don't you?"

"William, please, just listen to me for a second. Okay? Please," Mother managed to say. "It doesn't matter; it really doesn't. I don't care what happened today. I mean, I do care, but God will see us through this. I know He will. I...I'll get a job. I can work. Charlie...Charlie's old enough now to be on his own. He doesn't need me hanging around here all day, driving him nuts. I'll start looking tomorrow, and Billy won't mind if he has to sit out for a semester or—"

"No, Claire, let me finish what I'm trying to tell you. You don't understand. Ed didn't *fire* me today—he *promoted* me! He gave me a raise, even made me vice-president over sales! Jon is quitting, moving to Jackson. He's been offered this big political job up there as Deputy Director of the State Insurance Commission. Turns out, he's the one who suggested to Ed I take over all his responsibilities at work! Can you believe it?"

I wasn't the least bit surprised. The only thing that surprised me about what Dad had just said was Mother didn't keel over in her plate of spaghetti and meatballs.

She didn't, but her jaw dropped. I don't know if Mother believed my dad, at first. She probably thought she was just dreaming or maybe Dad was joking, but I didn't. I knew he was telling the truth because I knew how and why it had happened. I just didn't expect my second request to be answered so soon. To be dead, those spirits certainly did move fast.

Mother jumped up from her chair and almost knocked it over. She ran around the table to Dad and planted a long, smothering kiss on his lips. Then she hugged Dad so hard he had to shove her away to keep her from choking him.

"Lord, Claire, what's gotten into you?" Dad blushed as badly as I did when Candy Watts ran out on the baseball field and planted a whopper on my lips after I had just hit a home run, the summer before in Tupelo. So I knew how he felt.

"William, I just can't believe it!" Mother exclaimed. I'm so proud of you I can hardly contain myself!"

"Thanks, Claire, but don't be proud of me. Truth is, I haven't done a thing. This is what's so hard for me to grasp, you know? I mean, why me? Why did Jon recommend *me* to Ed? I never even thought Jon wanted Ed to hire me."

"But you said yourself, just last night, Ed liked you a lot—he thought you had, what were his words…?"

" 'Excellent potential,' " I reminded Mother.

"That's right. Thanks, Charlie. Excellent potential."

"Well, even so, I just can't figure why Ed would have given *me* such a big promotion and raise, so soon. After all, I've only been there… Claire, there're *several* people at the agency who deserve Jon's job more than I do—like Jerry Latimer, for instance. He's been there almost three years. It just doesn't seem fair to Jerry or to… Frankly, Claire, I'm embarrassed—"

Mother kissed Dad on the mouth again and forced him to shut up. Though it truly was a revolting sight, I was glad. Now it was my turn. I would merely smile, lean back in my chair, fold my arms behind my head, and tell them both the reason why Dad would now be making more money in his new job. But they might not believe me at first, so I rehearsed my story.

It was simple. The spirits were so grateful I had found their old gold coin, which they had lost, they granted my second request. Surely, Mother and Dad could understand this. And Hank had been right: Dad definitely did "get it."

But before I could proceed, there was a loud pounding on the front door, almost like there was someone outside trying to kick it in.

"Billy!" I hollered. "He's finally here!"

"Get up and go help him, Charlie," Mother said. "He probably can't turn the knob with the suitcases in his hands."

I got up so fast from the table I knocked my glass of milk over. "Sorry!" I yelled over my shoulder back to my mother as I ran from the dining room and into the den. "I'm coming!" I twisted the doorknob and jerked open the door…

But it wasn't Billy. It was Malachi the cop, whom I had encountered the night before.

Malachi was holding Tillman's hand, and Tillie and Hank were standing behind them.

Tillman's head was slightly bowed, but I could still tell he had been crying about something. I didn't know what Tillman had done, but it was obviously bad.

No one was smiling. I did feel sorry for Tillman, but I hadn't done anything—so what were they doing at *our* house?

"Hello, again, Charlie Hall," Malachi said to me. He managed a faint smile on his broad, black face. "Do you remember me?"

"Yes, sir," I said, hesitantly.

"Mind if we come inside?"

"Uh, I guess not, but I better go ask my parents…" This wasn't necessary, though. From their chairs, both Dad and Mother had a clear view of the front door, and when they saw a police officer standing there holding Tillman's hand like he was in trouble or something, they both got up from the table and had already come to the door by the time I had turned around to go ask them if Malachi the cop could come inside.

When I saw them standing behind me, I stepped away from the door. Dad's arms were folded. Mother looked very concerned.

Tillman's head was still bowed. It was like he was too embarrassed or afraid to even look at me. He started crying. Tears as big as raindrops were falling from his eyes onto the door sill. Hank was standing directly behind Tillman. He reached up and put his big hand on Tillman's shoulder. "It's okay, Tillman. Try not to cry, all right? Remember what I said to you before we left the house? It's time now to finally be a man."

"Is there something wrong, Officer?" my dad asked Malachi.

"What's happened?" Mother asked him, nervously.

Still with a faint smile on his face, Malachi looked at them both, but I could tell his smile was more practiced, more routine, than real. "Mr. and Mrs. Hall, I'm Sergeant Malachi Jones, Natchez Police Department. I think y'all probably know Tillman

Dawes, here."

Mother, Dad, and I all nodded at precisely the same time, like those three monkeys that don't approve of anything evil.

Sergeant Jones motioned with his head toward Hank and Tillie behind him. "And these here folks are your neighbors who Tillman stays with, in the big old house across the—"

"Yes," Mother said, "Tillie and I are friends." Dad and Mother were both staring at Hank, though, since they had no idea who or what he was.

"Do y'all mind if we come in?" Sergeant Jones asked. "It's, uh, important."

"No, I mean, yes, yes—of course," Mother said. "Please, come on in."

As Sergeant Jones and Tillman walked in, Mother and Dad looked at me, sternly. It was apparent they both assumed Tillman and I had perpetrated some juvenile offense and we were both in trouble, but I knew I was clean. And if Tillman had lied to this cop and implicated me, I was going to give him the beating of his life. I shrugged my shoulders at my parents to try to assure them both I had no idea what this matter was all about. Sergeant Jones let go of Tillman's hand, and Tillman walked over and hugged me. I could smell cigarettes on him, and I tried to push him away, but he wouldn't let go of me. "Stop it, Tillman!" I said coldly to him. "Stop it, you…you *weirdo*!" I shoved him hard and broke free.

Tillman stumbled a couple of steps backwards. He looked at me with tears in his sad, green eyes and said, "Charlie, I'm…I'm sorry. I'm so sorry. I really am."

"Yeah, I bet you are, Tillman! What have you done

now? Huh? What lie have you told this cop? *What?*" I looked at Sergeant Jones with both anger and fear. "Whatever Tillman's told you is a lie! It's all he ever does is lie and make up—"

"Tillman's not lying about anything, Charlie," Hank stepped forward and said. "This is not about you or him. It's about your brother, Billy. There's been an accident. A bad one."

"Oh, my God!" Mother exclaimed as she put her hands to her mouth. "Oh, no, no…"

Dad didn't say anything, but both his arms went limp at his sides, like he had just been shot again in the butt.

Mother kept shaking her head and saying, "No, no, no…"

Tillie walked over to Mother and hugged her around the neck. Mother hugged her back tightly and began to weep.

Hank walked up to Dad and introduced himself. My father was pallid, stunned. Hank had to lift Dad's right arm to shake his hand. He probably never even heard Hank say who he was, much less cared. Dad's brain may have been racing, but his heart and soul had just died. "Is Billy, is he—"

"No, your son is still alive," Sergeant Jones advised us.

"Oh, thank God, thank God!" Mother said. She and Tillie let go of each other. "Praise God!" Mother said, again.

"He was conscious when the ambulance brought him to the hospital. But I need to let you all know…it was a bad wreck. Your son wasn't wearing a seat belt. He was thrown through the windshield. His head was fractured, and there's probably a lot of internal damage—"

"When did it happen?" Dad asked, mechanically. "Where did it happen?"

"About five o'clock, three miles north of town on Highway 61. I happened to be near there when I heard it on my radio. I got there just before the ambulance—"

"Where have they taken him?" Mother asked, frantically. "I want to see my son. *Now*!"

"He's at Memorial Hospital, Mrs. Hall. That's why I'm here. Y'all can follow me there."

Tillie hugged my mother, again. "We'll stay here with Charlie," she told her.

"No!" I shouted. "I'm going, too! Billy's my brother. I want to go see him. I'm not staying here with them. I'm not! I'm not! I'm…" The den started spinning around and around.

Instantly, I had a flashback to the dream I'd had, early the same morning, before Dad had knocked on my door and told me to come to breakfast.

In my mind, I could see Billy as clearly as I saw my dad standing next to me. Billy was sitting on his bike, at the top of the hill, smiling down at me. His blue eyes radiated with love, a love so strong it was blinding. And he looked so happy, so at peace. Like a baby in his mother's arms, staring up at her face.

Then, just like in my dream, Billy cupped both his hands to his mouth and hollered down to me, "Charlie…it's *beautiful* up here! You have to see this! Sis is here, too!"

I hollered back to him, "Wait for me, Billy! I'm pedaling as fast as I can!"

Billy yelled back, "Don't worry, Charlie, I'm not

going anywhere! I'm never gonna leave you, never gonna leave you, never gonna—"

"He lied to me!" I blurted out, as I suddenly realized the meaning of my dream. I looked desperately at Mother. "Don't you understand? Billy lied to me in my dream! He promised me he'd never leave me, but he did. He lied to me…!"

I fell to my knees onto the hard floor, bent over, and began sobbing as my whole world began to fall apart around me. I was devastated, hysterical, dying inside. My breaths were quick and short, like a sudden panic attack had just happened to me. *So this is what it feels like to die*, I recall telling myself.

My mother started to come to me, but Tillie stopped her. "No, Claire, no. Let Charlie be. You and William need to go. We'll take care of Charlie. Go be with Billy now. Hurry."

Mother looked at Tillie and started to speak.

"Go," Tillie said, again. "Go now."

Tillie let go of my mother's arm. Mother walked over to where I was hunched over on the floor. She kneeled and hugged me, and she kissed me on top of my head. "Pray, Charlie, okay? Pray for God's will. Just pray God's will for Billy—"

"No! I don't care about God's will! I want Billy to be healed! I want him to be with me forever, like he promised!" I never even looked at my mother.

Dad reached inside his blue blazer on the coat rack and got his keys. He walked over to Mother and helped her off the floor. "We need to go now, Claire. Charlie'll be okay here."

****

It all seemed like a nightmare from hell after this,

and there's a lot I've chosen not to remember, but this is what I recall:

After Sergeant Jones and my parents drove off, I must have fallen asleep. I awoke and heard Tillie say something to Hank about helping her clear the table away and putting the leftover spaghetti and meatballs in the refrigerator for my parents, in case they were hungry when they returned home.

It was probably eight-thirty, by then. I was still down on the floor in the den, curled up in a fetal position next to the sofa and praying I could fall back asleep and never wake up. I realized, even at thirteen, I had to accept the harsh reality of what had happened, but it was impossible. Death itself seemed better to me than life without my beloved brother Billy.

Mother had asked me to pray for God's will before she and Dad left. But God's will for what—Billy to survive but be disabled for the rest of his life? No, no! This was not acceptable.

I knew Billy too well. He was too proud, too full of life, to ever want to live the rest of his life that way. Billy would have preferred God's will to be for him to die, I remember thinking.

But I just couldn't. It was unbearable to think of my tough, brave, devil-may-care brother, who had always looked after and protected me, being disabled for the rest of his life. But I loved Billy too much to ever let him go.

There just had to be another answer, and then I realized what I had to do to ensure Billy would be healed.

The answer was as simple as it was obvious.

I slowly stood up from the floor and took a deep,

long breath. I was rubbing both my eyes when Tillie noticed me standing in the den. After she and Hank had cleared all the plates and everything from the dining room table, Tillie was removing the tablecloth soiled from the milk I had spilled earlier.

"Did you get enough to eat, Charlie? There's plenty of spaghetti and French bread left. If you're hungry, I can—"

"No, ma'am. I don't want any more spaghetti, and I hate Mother's meatballs."

Tillie draped the tablecloth over the back of a chair and tried to wipe the moisture dry with a cloth napkin so the table wouldn't be stained. "How about some milk and chocolate cookies, then? Assuming Hank hasn't eaten all of them, by now," she said. "He happened to discover an opened bag of those cookies in your pantry, next to the refrigerator."

"No, ma'am. Hank can have them all. I know how much he and the spirits like chocolate. Where's Tillman?"

"I sent him home. He said to please tell you again how sorry he is about what happened."

"Tillie, I don't know why I said all those mean things to Tillman. I really don't. I, I just thought he'd probably gotten me in some kinda trouble. Will you please tell him I'm—"

"I know, Charlie. I know. You were just scared. Tillman understands. He fibs a lot, I know this, but it's not really his fault when you consider his background. Tillman's just insecure, but he has a very tender heart. He always has. He's already forgiven you. Charlie?"

"Yes, ma'am?"

"I need to talk to you about Billy."

"Sure, but I need to talk to you about him first."

"Okay…okay." Tillie draped the linen napkin over the back of another chair. She looked into the kitchen and spoke to Hank. "Don't eat all those chocolate cookies, Hank. Save some for Charlie, you hear me?"

"Sorry, Tillie, too late," I heard Hank say. "I'm doing the dishes now. They don't have a damn dishwasher, and they have the ugliest yellow refrigerator I've ever—"

"Good. It's your penance for being such a boozer…a glutton, too!" Tillie looked back at me and motioned with her hand. "Let's you and I have a seat in the den, on your couch."

Tillie and I sat down on Mother's sofa, side by side. She bowed her head and rubbed her hands together, like she was in deep thought, maybe praying. Then she looked up at the ceiling and sighed heavily. Tillie started to say something to me, but I stopped her.

"It's okay, Tillie. Everything's going to be okay now. I know it is. You don't have to worry about Billy anymore. I promise you don't."

"I'm not worried about Billy, Charlie; I'm worried about you." Tillie's response and the look on her face surprised me.

"Me? Why? I'm fine," I told her.

"What was it you wanted to say to me about Billy?"

"I know he's gonna be healed. Billy's gonna be okay, Tillie. I just know he is."

"How do you know this?"

"You know how, Tillie…your spirit friends! They can do anything. They've already proved it to me, twice. Just today, they caused Dad to get promoted and make more money at his new job. Just like Hank guaranteed they would, this very morning. He told me my father would get it, and he definitely—"

"Charlie, what is it you want the spirits to do for you and for Billy?" She put her hand on my knee and started patting it, like she had done the previous night.

"Don't you already know? I can't believe you just asked me this, Tillie. I want Billy to be healed. Right now."

"*Physically* healed?"

"Of course. What else is there?"

"If Billy were physically healed, Charlie, what do you think he would do?"

"He'd be Billy again. Duh."

"Okay," she said. "What else do you want from the spirits?"

I shook my head and tried to think. "I…I really don't know. Isn't this enough?"

"No, there's something else. Something I heard you say to your parents before they left."

"I don't remember."

"Yes, you do, Charlie. It was something you said Billy had promised you. Try to remember."

I thought for a moment. "Yeah, yeah, now I remember! He promised me in a dream I had, right before I woke up this morning, that he'd never leave me. That was it!"

Tillie squeezed my knee, and then she removed her hand. She put her long arm around my shoulder, drew me close to her, and kissed me on the top of my head. "Very well, then, your third request, *both* of them, are granted. And just like you asked for, Charlie: Right now."

"Right now?"

"Isn't this what you wanted?"

"Well, yeah, sure, but I, I don't—"

"Don't what?"

"I don't have a third *gift* to give them. I don't have anything else. Hank ate the rest of the chocolate cookies."

Tillie smiled. She hugged me and kissed my blond hair again.

"I have some very good news for you, Charlie Hall, some *excellent* news! This time the third gift is for *you.* It's from the spirits—and from Billy, too."

Tillie was talking nonsense. I didn't understand what she meant, but something inside me told me to run, run away, as fast and far as I could. But I had nowhere to go. Where *could* I go? I was already in my own house, and so was she.

"What are you trying to tell me, Tillie? What kind of gift could Billy be giving *me*? He's in the hospital, right? Right, Tillie? Tillie…?"

"Charlie, I need to tell you what I started to tell you a while ago, before we sat down. Do you recall last night, out on our front porch, after that nice young couple, the Feltons, had left, and Tillman came outside and joined us? Do you remember how sad he was about their daughter drowning? How hard he had been crying? And do you remember what I told Tillman?"

I had no intention of even answering Tillie, much less accepting what I knew she was about to say. I couldn't even look at her, anymore. It was all I could stand, just to be sitting on the same sofa with her, to even be in the same room with her. Yes, I remembered what she had told Tillman. But Tillie was wrong. She was wrong! *She just had to be…*

"That, sometimes, after a person dies, they're closer to us than they ever were before—"

"No! No!" I jumped up from the sofa and screamed in her face. "You're lying, Tillie! You're a liar, too—just like Tillman! This can't be true…it just can't be! You promised me, Tillie. You just promised me! You promised me Billy was healed, and he'd—"

"Charlie, Charlie…Billy *is* healed."

Hank came walking quickly into the den. "Charlie?" he said. "What's the matter?"

"And he'd never leave me! You promised me, Tillie! You—"

The front door opened, slowly. My mother and father were standing there, pallid and weary, and I could tell they had been crying. They both seemed emotionally and physically exhausted, almost lifeless. I assumed they had probably heard me yelling at Tillie before they walked inside the house, but I knew this wasn't the problem. My worst fear had just become a reality. Mother started to say something to Tillie, Hank, and me, but I didn't want to hear it. I couldn't. I already knew what it was. Without speaking to anyone, I ran out of the den and down the hall into my bedroom. I slammed the door behind me.

****

I've never understood why, but Mississippians—perhaps all Southerners—have an innate propensity to gravitate into the kitchen to visit, gossip, party, fight, and, sometimes, just to cry. There was a lot of crying in our kitchen Tuesday night—mainly by Mother and Dad, I was told—but also by both Tillie and Hank. They talked late into the night, while the four of them stood around and consumed a lot of black coffee and cigarettes.

Hank begged my parents to let him warm the leftover spaghetti and French bread and to make them another salad, but my parents said they weren't hungry. Hank's strong coffee and four empathetic ears were all Mother and Dad said they wanted or needed, at the time.

The next day, I learned Dad told Tillie and Hank that witnesses claimed Billy wasn't speeding, but he had swerved his Ford to miss a deer in the middle of the highway, exactly where Sergeant Jones said the accident occurred. The car had left the road and flipped a couple times, throwing Billy through the windshield and into a tree. When the ambulance crew arrived, they could clearly see Billy had an extensive head injury, but they didn't realize how much he was damaged internally, until they brought him to the hospital. Dad also told Hank and Tillie there were several opened cans of beer found inside the car.

Dad said when he and Mother arrived at the hospital with Sergeant Jones, Billy had already been taken into surgery. The physician on call, Dr. Kirk O'Brien, told them later that, as soon as their son was rolled in, he knew immediately Billy had internal trauma, and he was probably bleeding profusely. He knew he had to perform emergency surgery to stop the bleeding, since this was more critical than his head injury. Dr. O'Brien said he and his staff tried desperately to keep Billy awake while they took him up the elevator and rolled him down the hall to the operating room to prep him for surgery, but Billy had lapsed into a coma.

The young trauma surgeon explained he had no other choice than to operate. He said he knew, from his experiences as an Army surgeon in Vietnam, if he didn't stop the bleeding internally, Billy would die within a few minutes.

As humanely as he could, he told my parents that when he cut open Billy's abdomen, the extent of damage to most of Billy's major organs was far worse than he had expected. He was able to stop the bleeding, he said, but this was all he could do. He then told them he needed their consent before the ambulance could transfer Billy a hundred miles north to the Level 1 Trauma Center at the University Hospital in Jackson, so he was glad they had finally arrived. Time was "of the essence," he said.

Mother told Dr. O'Brien she wanted to see her son. He warned her and Dad Billy's face and skull were severely damaged and he probably wouldn't be aware of their presence, but they didn't care. He led them into the recovery room, where Billy was lying motionless on a bed, shielded from view by three curtains.

When a nurse retracted one of the curtains, my parents said they were horrified at what they saw. There were two tubes with needles stuck into Billy's arms, which ran to two vinyl pouches with a clear liquid in each, hanging from metal poles next to Billy's bed. There were also two machines next to the head of Billy's bed, with red and green flashing lights, which were attached to Billy's chest by suction cups and plastic wires.

They saw an oxygen mask covering what was still recognizable of Billy's once handsome face. A heart monitor, attached to Billy's chest, was connected to another machine which was beeping, indicating Billy was still fighting for the life he had always hated, but a life I had always loved and admired. Then they saw the long scar on his swollen belly, which had been hastily stitched by Dr. Kirk O'Brien.

I was told it was all my mother and dad could do to approach their dying son, and Mother told Tillie the four-foot walk to Billy's bed was like walking to the electric chair. Mother went to one side of Billy's bed, and Dad went to the other. They each held one of Billy's hands in theirs. The nurse closed the blue curtain behind them and left, so William and Claire Hall could be alone with their oldest son, one last time.

Then Mother told Tillie the oddest thing happened. Instead of breaking down, crying, and begging God to spare Billy's life, like she assumed she would, she said she felt the most amazing peace she had ever known. When she saw Billy lying in a bed, all crushed and scarred physically, she said she somehow knew his spirit was healed, happy, alive. And at peace.

Just like *she* finally was.

She said she sensed Billy was about to die, so the transfer up to Jackson would be in vain. Mother said that when she looked over at my father and saw him in such agonizing torment and fear, she mainly felt sadness for him.

She leaned over and kissed Billy on his badly scarred and swollen forehead, and as she stroked his bloodstained, curly blond hair, she spoke to him softly. "I love you, Billy. Your dad and I both do. Charlie's so upset…you know how much he's always worshipped you. Before you go, I want you—I *beg* you—to promise me two things: Please keep looking after

Charlie, just like you've always done, and please, please forgive me for what I did to you. I never meant to hurt you, Billy. I'm so very sorry. I never meant to hurt you, son."

Dad said he never saw this happen, but Mother swore Billy opened his blue eyes, smiled, and gently squeezed her hand. Then he closed his eyes and died.

****

Right before Tillie and Hank left, Mother told Dad she couldn't bear to telephone Grandmother Justice and tell her what had happened. Dad said he would do this for her, and he would call the other members of both their families, as well. Dad said he also needed to call Ed and advise him what had happened and that he would be up in Tupelo the rest of the week for Billy's funeral. Mother asked Dad to also call some of Billy's friends in Tupelo and Canon Long, up at Ole Miss.

She told him to be sure to tell Canon to *not* call Ann Marie, but to go to where she lived and be there personally when he told her what had happened. Mother said her primary concern, at the moment, was for Ann Marie, and to tell Canon to have Ann Marie call her, collect.

Mother said Tillie asked her if she could look in on me before she and Hank left. Mother suggested they both go check on me. She said they walked down the hall to my bedroom and opened the door. The light was still on. I had never undressed and had cried myself to sleep.

Mother said she started to walk over to the bed to kiss me, but Tillie put out her arm and stopped her. "No, Claire, not now," Tillie told my mother. "Let's not disturb him. Let him keep on sleeping. Please trust me.

You kiss him later, for me too." They closed the door and left.

My mother said she thought this was odd, but she did what Tillie told her. After all, she already knew Sharon Tillman Dawes spoke the truth.

Epilogue

I remember the summer of 1978 as a distant, one-night dream. Most folks claim time heals all wounds, but I think they're wrong. Some wounds never heal because love never dies. Time merely covers them up, like coats of paint on the outside of an old wooden house.

Time, I've come to believe, is the great tester of hope and faith.

Change has always been hard for me. When I discussed this one night with my fiancée, Sarah, who's both beautiful and wise, she informed me change is hard for most people. I guess she's probably right. And I recalled Hank once quoting an old Greek philosopher who wrote, "All is flux, nothing stays still; there is nothing permanent except change." How I desperately tried to resist this major change in my life, though. How I prayed we could all go back to *before* my card house was smashed flat, like Billy had smashed his, one Thanksgiving day in Tupelo.

The days, weeks, and months following this horrible Tuesday night in May were almost unbearable. The only way I survived was to hide from other people, God, and even myself.

I avoided Tillie and Hank completely, and I didn't go to their house again. I only saw Tillman in passing, the rest of the summer. When school started the following September, I would sometimes nod at Tillman when I saw him in the hall. Sometimes, I would not. We rarely, if ever, spoke again, but I was popular and studied and made good grades. Just like Tillie and her spirit friends had promised I would.

My father escaped by throwing himself into his job, and, in January of 1979, he bought a nicer and bigger-than-needed house in a fancy neighborhood on the other side of Natchez. My mother was the only one who didn't want to leave, since she and Tillie had become close friends. Dad said the change would do us all good, but, again, I somehow knew he really meant himself.

After Dad ran from those damn North Koreans, I guess he just never learned how to stop.

This was also when I left Montebello Junior High School and started attending a private school with rich kids I never really liked and who never liked me. My grades stunk, but I played baseball there and was pretty good at it. I also fell in love there and soon became a man.

I've always regretted never apologizing to Tillman for those mean things I said to him, the night Billy died. Once, though, when I was a senior, and I'd had a little too much to drink, I recalled how Tillman hugged me, after he came inside with Sergeant Jones, and how sad he had been. Tillman was the better man. Like Tillie and Hank both said, Tillman had a great heart.

Tillman graduated from Mississippi State with honors and moved to Wilmore, Kentucky to attend Asbury Theological Seminary. His first year there, Hank died from emphysema, so Tillman, I learned from Mother, insisted Tillie sell her home and come live with him, his wife, and their new son, named "Hank." I was a senior at Ole Miss, then, and was home for Easter break.

This was also when I asked Mother if she had any idea what had become of Ann Marie. The only time I had met her was when everyone was sitting around the parlor, before the funeral, talking about Billy. Mother said that, after Billy's funeral and his burial next to Sis's grave at the cemetery were over, she never heard from her again. I really didn't blame Ann Marie for never contacting our family again, though. I knew how hard it was to try to forgive and forget.

The day before I left Natchez to drive back to Oxford, Tillie called our house and asked to speak to me. I started not to take the call, but Mother begged me to talk to her, so I did. Tillie asked if I would please come by her home for a short visit. There was "something important," she said, she needed to tell me.

I didn't want to go, but there was something in her voice which was compelling, intriguing, and something in me said if I didn't, I would never know the real truth.

I drove up and down Melrose Avenue three or four times. It had been several years since I had been on the street. I was surprised how little it had changed, while I had changed so much.

The cheap, ugly brick on our old house had been painted white, but other than this it still looked the same. Tillie's home needed painting, though, and the grass needed cutting, just like it always did. And it had a big For Sale sign in the front yard. I finally stopped and parked my car in the driveway. I got out, and I slowly walked up the rickety front steps.

When I turned the old doorbell key, Tillie yelled

from the left front parlor and told me to come inside.

Even the smell was still the same. I knew Tillie was too old to still smoke, but I distinctly smelled cigarettes and immediately thought of Hank. Tillie was sitting on the faded, green velvet sofa in the middle of the room, and she patted her hand on it for me to come sit next to her. She was sipping black coffee from one of Hank's New Orleans Saints mugs, and she asked me if I would like some. I told her no, since I still didn't drink coffee, and that I couldn't stay too long. Tillie looked so old and decrepit I wanted to cry.

"Okay," Tillie said, "but there's something I want you to know, Charlie. I didn't lie to you the night your brother died; I didn't."

I stared into her brown, aged eyes, not knowing what to say or having the slightest idea what Tillie was talking about.

It had been several years since we had talked, but I could tell Tillie knew what I was thinking. "You don't remember, do you, Charlie?"

I was grown, educated, and considered myself worldly, but I was still naïve. Perhaps even worse, still emotionally detached. I shook my head. "No, I'm afraid I don't, Tillie. Just what are you referring to?" I cautiously asked her.

"The night your brother Billy died…you and I were sitting on the couch in your den, and I promised you Billy was healed and that he'd never leave you."

I was appalled Tillie could be so insensitive, to bring up such a painful memory, one I had tried so long and hard to forget, for the past eight years. "I need to be going now," I curtly told her. "I have a long drive back to Oxford, and I have a big test tomorrow in—"

"No, not yet. We'll never have this chance again, and you need to know the truth. Billy *was* healed, just not how you thought. He was emotionally and spiritually healed, and Billy didn't leave you, Charlie. He's never left you, and he never will.

"You had already gone to bed. Your mama and I went back to your room so she could kiss you. She started to walk over to your bed, but I stopped her when I saw him."

I remember thinking Tillie was probably senile, or perhaps irrational from living alone for so long. I knew I probably shouldn't have, but I asked her to explain. "Saw who, Tillie? Who did you see in my room?"

"Billy's spirit," she said. "He was sitting there on the side of your bed, rubbing your blond hair as you slept. He looked so happy and at peace, but I sensed he was worried about you. He was trying to console you, Charlie. So I told your mama not to wake you up."

I knew I had to leave immediately, to run away, like my dad. I was starting to get tears in my eyes, and I couldn't let this happen. I couldn't let myself remember, again. It was too hard to forget. I stood up from her sofa and tried to change the subject as quickly as I could. "I certainly hope your home sells soon and all these valuable antiques and heirlooms you own, too."

"It's already sold," she told me, "the contents and all. And you were right, Charlie—it *is* just a bunch of 'old junk.' "

I extended my hand to her and tried to feign a smile. "I wish you all the best, Tillie. I sincerely do. And I was so sorry to hear about Hank. I was always quite fond of him."

"Thanks. Hank was always quite fond of you, too."

"Please tell Tillman hello," I told her. "It's been so long since—"

"Yes, much too long since you both talked. You and me, too." Tillie set her Saints coffee mug on the end table next to her and stood. She gave me a long hug. I was too tall for her to kiss me on my hair anymore, so she pushed back with both her arms and smiled at me. "I just can't believe how much you've grown and what a fine, handsome young man you've become."

"Thank you," I told her politely. "I have to go now."

"I know," Tillie said, "but before you leave, Charlie, there is one more thing I need to say to you first."

"Tillie, please, I really do have to be—"

"Your third gift, the one to you from the spirits and from Billy, too—he promised he'd always look after you. He has. He's standing next to you right now, smiling at us both."

I stepped backwards, and Tillie let go of my arms. I had nothing more to say to her, and I didn't want to hear any more. I turned and walked quickly away, never looking back.

This was the last time I ever saw her. I drove back to Ole Miss that afternoon, and after Tillie sold her home and all its contents, she moved away to Kentucky to live with Tillman.

Tillman got my telephone number from my mother, and he called me a couple years later. I had received my marketing degree by then and was working in Jackson, Mississippi as a copywriter for an advertising agency. He told me how good it was to hear my voice again and not to get married too soon, like he had done.

I asked him about his wife and family. He had two sons, now, he told me, Hank and Tillman, Jr., and he and his wife, Lisa, were still very much in love. Tillman never did become a preacher but decided, instead, to become a Christian counselor. He loved his work, he said, especially working with families who had just lost loved ones and with spouses who had been recently divorced. I told Tillman I was glad to hear this, since he had a sensitive heart and spirit, just like Tillie. I also told Tillman how happy I was for him.

Then he said Tillie had died and they had buried her up there. I told Tillman I was sorry to hear this and thanked him for letting me know. We wished each other well and promised to stay in touch before we finally hung up, but I knew we probably wouldn't. I left my office, walked down a flight of stairs to the men's room, looked under all three stall doors, opened one of them, and locked it. Then I sat down on the commode cover and cried.

I've often remembered the last time I saw Tillie Dawes and everything she told me. And who knows— maybe she *did* see Billy's spirit sitting on the side of my bed, rubbing my hair, and trying to console me. Just like he had always done.

All I know is, it's exactly what I dreamed that night.

I should have told Tillie about my dream. But I was too afraid to remember, too afraid to have to try to forget about Billy, all over again. So it was actually I who lied to her.

Somehow, though, I think Tillie knows and

understands. She always did know me better than I knew myself. Perhaps she still does.

When Sarah and I drove to Natchez one Christmas to spend the holidays with my folks, I decided late Christmas night, after drinking a few Jim-Beam-and-Cokes with Dad, to drive Sarah past Tillie's old home, which I had often told her about. Sarah didn't care to see it and wanted to go to bed, but I told her I didn't want to go by myself, so she agreed.

The place looked totally different. It had been refurbished on the outside and had been painted a pastel green. The grass had been cut as neatly as a golf course, and the front yard was landscaped with crape myrtle trees, magnolias, and an array of azalea and camellia bushes.

There was a full moon out that evening, and the front porch was suffused in light. Inside, though, the house was dark, so we assumed the new owners had left Natchez for the holidays. I stopped my new truck, lowered my window, and lit a Marlboro Light for a long, reflective look.

Maybe it was just my imagination, or maybe it was all the Jim-Beam-and-Cokes, but I told Sarah I thought I saw Tillie dancing naked on the front porch again, swirling around in the bright, silver moonlight to the tune of some haunting refrain—the melody of her heartbeat.

Sarah said she never saw her, that I had obviously had too much to drink, and it was time to go back home. Sarah was right, I did have too much to drink with Dad, but she was also wrong. It was like Dad told my mother: "Some things have to be believed to be seen."

A word about the author…

David Armstrong was born and raised in Natchez, Mississippi, and is a former mayor and recovering attorney. *The Third Gift* is David's second novel. His first novel, *The Rising Place*, was also published by The Wild Rose Press and has been made into a feature film.

David has also written four screenplays, and when he isn't working his daytime job as the COO for the City of Columbus, Mississippi, he is working on two other novels.

He is the father of two grown sons and lives in one of the oldest and most haunted antebellum homes in Columbus with a crazy cat named Butch.

Find him at:
www.therisingplace.com

Thank you for purchasing
this publication of The Wild Rose Press, Inc.

For questions or more information
contact us at
info@thewildrosepress.com.

The Wild Rose Press, Inc.
www.thewildrosepress.com

www.ingramcontent.com/pod-product-compliance
Lightning Source LLC
Chambersburg PA
CBHW060551260626
47161CB00003B/1146